TRULY, MADLY, STEEPLY, BREW

Truly, Madly, Steeply Brew

This is a work of fiction. Any mention of names, places, and characters is fiction and for entertainment purposes only.

Not liable for any sudden coffee cravings which occur while reading this book.

Contents

Introduction

Welcome to the Autumn-perfect, Christmas-perfect, and falling-in-love-perfect town of Mapleton, Vermont. If this is your first trip to town, sit back and prepare for fun banter and shenanigans to bring you all the feels. If you are returning to Mapleton, welcome home.

Welcome to Mapleton, Vermont

One

Arielle Hanson

Yanking on the wrought iron door handle of the Long Island Coffee Loft, I storm through the entry with so much anger bubbling in my gut, my gaze has morphed into tunnel vision. I barely pause to scan the lobby, making sure it's clear of customers before I zero my gaze on my brother, Christian, and shriek, "Tom *is* lying. He has another girlfriend!"

Portia, Christian's fiancée, pops up from where she was restocking supplies behind the counter. Her snow-blond hair is pinned in a messy bun, making her look like she hasn't combed it for the day, but that doesn't slow her down. She immediately paces toward me, hands outstretched. "That dirty scumbag."

I stand with my feet shoulder width apart, but still feel increasing weakness in my knees. Portia wraps her arms around me, and I drop my head on her shoulder and sob, unleashing a flood of tears.

Christian strides forward, determination in his straight path to us. "Are you *sure* this time?"

I raise my head enough to catch his gaze. He's the one person I'm totally honest with, and I desperately need consoling on this. "Yeah. You know how I had suspected it, but he assured me so many times that was not the case? He always had perfectly reasonable excuses why we had to sneak around. Remember when he said he was a lawyer, who worked at the same law firm handling Grandma's estate, and he was worried about the conflict of interest?"

Christian's eyes narrow, red hues flaming on his cheeks. "Tell me he's at least a lawyer."

"He's a lawyer." I nod, sniffing back tears. "Yet, still a liar."

Christian's hands roll into fists and his lips snarl and twist to the side. "I'll show him what a loser he really is."

"No, I don't want him to know how much this bothers me." I place my hand on his shoulder, attempting to take his fury down a notch. "I'm ready to never hear his voice or see his face again."

"How did you get him to confess?" Portia stares at me, her eyes wide with piqued interest.

"He never confessed but nothing ever added up. Today is his birthday, and he said he didn't have time to get together. I offered to meet him for lunch at his work, but he didn't want me to come to the office. I thought that was weird, but he assured me he was concerned over the conflict of interest. I showed up anyway—"

"You did not!" Portia's jaw practically drops to the floor.

"I did." I swipe my eyes with the back of my hands, doing everything I can to restore my vision as Portia's sweet face blurs in front of me. "That's what you do when you love someone and it's their birthday. I understood he was busy, but I thought I could still drop off a birthday lunch and give him a hug and kiss. But when I got there, he was having lunch in his office *with his other girlfriend!*"

Portia gasps, covering her mouth with her palm. "She was there?"

"It was a good thing too." I don't conceal the exasperation layering in my tone. I've been holding it in the entire drive here. If I don't let it out, my emotional tank is going to explode. "Tom would have never fessed up. At least since his other girlfriend was literally right there in front of my face, there was no way to lie his way out of it."

"I'm so sorry." Portia squeezes me tighter and pats my back in a motherly way. "He really doesn't deserve you. I know this hurts, but it's better you find out now. You should be with someone who treats you the way you deserve."

My bottom lip rolls under until I trap it between my teeth. I want to believe she's right, and there is someone better out there for me, but I'm honestly so tired of dating. I stopped looking for the perfect guy years ago. He just doesn't exist, and if I had to be honest with myself, I know I was settling with Tom. It's part of my personality though, which I have an impossible time giving up. I don't like to admit defeat at anything, including relationships. I had desperately wanted to make this relationship work, because I'm ready to move on to the next stage of my life—to get married and have a family.

Growing up without a mom taught me a lot, but the loudest lesson it imparted to me is there are no guarantees. Life is short. My heart hollows fractionally more with each depressing thought until it lands on this last one. *I don't want to start all over again.* I'm gutted. I gave everything I had to Tom.

I can't do this again.

"I'll tell you what he deserves," Christian cuts in, wringing his fists together. The sight of him puffing up his chest, acting so tough should make me giggle, because Christian is the last guy to ever be physically aggressive, but I don't have even a snicker inside me.

"Violence is not the answer." Portia raises her gaze to lock with Christian's, but it's not scolding. She has a way of making him *even*. He immediately comes down another notch, unrolling his clenched fists.

"I agree." I sniff, finally straightening up with the bitter aftertaste of my dream of getting that Instagram-perfect wedding to disintegrate right before me. I take an urgent step back from Portia to look at Christian. "Violence will not help anything, but I can't go back there anytime soon. I was hoping I could stay with you for a little while."

"Stay here. Isn't that what you did the last time Tom hurt you?" Christian rubs his clean-shaven chin; a challenging gleam sparks in his eye. "I'm detecting a pattern where you always run away from your problems."

"It will not be a pattern once I get Tom out of my life for good. I'm humiliated. I can't imagine running into anyone I know right now, while I'm still so emotional." I sniff, and my shoulders shake from the internal pressure of holding back more tears. This isn't one of those problems I can solve by eating too many pints of ice cream and blaring Taylor Swift while I drive aimlessly around town.

This is my heart squeezed so tightly, it's impossible to breathe.

I've never been betrayed this badly before. I close my eyes, wishing the pain to go away, but Tom's face floods my mind, making my stomach lurch. I can't fathom ever feeling normal again.

I know one thing. If I do ever heal this pain, I'm not ever dating again.

This will not be my pattern.

I'm going to heal, but never date again. Problem solved.

"Don't you have a job to get back to?" Christian's protective-older-brother tone turns on. "I thought you had started cleaning for Dad's offices."

"I did, but it's just cleaning. It will not be the end of the world if I skip a week." I drop my voice into an indistinct murmur, adding under my breath, "Or a month." I can't afford to miss work with my dad, who's not exactly the understanding type. He'll more than likely "teach me a lesson" and fire me for not coming in. I'm willing to risk it, because as of right now, I can't imagine ever going back there. People are going to find out what I did—dating a guy with another girlfriend—and they'll talk. That's not my personality at all, but are they really going to believe that it wasn't my fault? I can't imagine the rumors going around about me. Nerves quake out of the depths of my gut, and I desperately motion to the counter. "I promise I'll earn my keep. I can take as many shifts as you want to help here."

"I actually just hired an assistant manager, Gia. She's not here right now, but she's working full time. With her new position, I really don't need any help, and I honestly can't afford it." Christian shrugs. His gaze bounces to Portia then back to me, all the while my heart sinks lower.

Is he really going to tell me I can't stay?

I get he has a life, but he's my older brother, who is *always* there for me.

"Christian." My voice is soft, cracking. "I don't have anyone back home but Dad, and I'm not ready to face him yet. He's going to throw it back into my face that I quit college to be with Tom and tell me all the ways I ruined my life. I know I messed up, but I can't hear that right now. Please—"

"I wasn't going to say no." He peers down at me, his words rushing out faster. "You didn't give me a chance. I was going to say I don't need help here, but I'm leaving on a business trip to acquire a new location. I'll only be gone for a couple of days to get the paperwork done. You're welcome to come with me."

"You're leaving?" I blink, and then blink again. Enough with my whining, this is great news! "I had no idea you were looking to expand. I would love to go anywhere as long as it's not back home." I jerk my thumb over my shoulder toward the parking lot. "My bag is already packed. We can take my car."

"That's fine." He nods, and his gaze trails back to Portia, who beams an approving smile.

"That's a wonderful idea, to have El come with you." She winks, and tacks on, "She'll keep you out of trouble."

"Yeah, it'll be good to have company for the drive, especially since I'm running late." He takes a step back, rubbing his chin. "I do need to request a loan pre-approval form from the bank before we head out, so if you'll excuse me a moment, I'll be ready to leave shortly."

"That's fine." I pace toward the nearest booth and plop down, staring at both my hands on the table. It's as if my body prefers to stay frozen.

"Can I get you something to drink?" Portia asks softly, her kindhearted smile aimed at me. "I'm partial to the French press."

I can't even fake a warm smile to repay her generosity. My heart is ripped open, but coffee sounds soothing. "Sure," I whimper as she turns on her heel to make my drink. I'm left to myself and it's overwhelming. I lay my head down and weep.

"Oh, honey." Portia comes from behind me and wraps both hands around me into another hug. "Please don't cry. He's not worth it. Trust me, I have a slew of men on my website who would love to meet you."

"Please don't even mention dating again." I shudder at her suggestion.

"I hate seeing you so upset over someone who clearly isn't worth it." Her kind eyes never leave my face as she rolls her bottom lip under her top teeth for a beat. Then she breaks the silence she created by rushing out, "If I let you in on a secret, do you promise not to say anything?"

"A secret about Tom?" My brows spring up, and my heart slams against my chest. "How do you have a secret?"

"No!" She pats my back, soothing me. "Not about Tom. This is something to cheer you up."

"No offense, Portia, but I just found out the love of my life was living a whole secret life. I really want to be miserable right now—"

"Stop!" She grabs both of my hands and squeezes them in a motherly way. "This isn't your fault and trust me," —she tosses a look over her shoulder before whispering— "This secret is so much fun, you can't be sad."

I slope my gaze up to her. "So, Christian doesn't even know?"

"He knows." She nods, dismissing my concern. "It's something I'm working on, and I haven't told many people because it's in beta."

"I don't know," I start slowly. After the worst day of my life having secrets being unveiled, I don't know if I can handle another secret. "You know what they say. Secrets are lies."

"This isn't a lie." She whips her phone out of her apron pocket and taps on the screen, and I immediately roll my eyes.

"I'm not going on your dating site—"

"It's not my matchmaking app." She slides her phone screen in front of me, and a bright blue screen flashes. "Karaoke Cash-oke," I read out loud, confusion bunching my brows together. "What is this?"

Her index finger taps her lips as she breathes out a quiet, "Shhh."

My eyes case side to side, confirming we're still alone. Unsure of why I need to be quiet. Unless that's just the presentation she does to drum up excitement for this thing. I give in and whisper, "What is this?"

"It's my new app." She taps the screen, and the app loads another screen where a personalized avatar with blond hair like hers pops up. A scoreboard floats above the avatar's head. "Like I said, it's still in beta," she explains. "I'm mostly just letting my paying clients from my other app get a free account here, but you pay to join these karaoke battles. I actually went out of my way to get a lottery license so I could upgrade the prizes, and now you can win real cash." She taps on the screen again, and a countdown starts on the top. "Here, try it."

"I didn't know you liked music." I take the phone from her, and stare at the brightly colored numbers, counting down from thirty seconds.

"Sure, everybody likes music, and it's just karaoke." Pointing to the screen again, her expression pulls into a serious one. "When that gets to zero, it's going to throw you into a round where you are randomly matched with another contestant. You battle it out, singing the same song."

"What?" My arm automatically stretches, thrusting the phone farther away from me. "I'm not in the mood to sing."

"It's so much fun." She pushes the phone closer to my face again. "Trust me, you will forget about what's his name."

The timer runs out, and the screen goes dark. My heart ticks up a notch. I have no idea what I'm doing. Bright red letters flash a song name, "I Will Survive," and I resist rolling my eyes on Portia. I know she's trying, but I just got done crying. I'm all nasally. "I'm not singing," I assert, crossing my arms across my chest.

"It's starting." Portia wags her index finger at the screen. "Please just try it this one time, and if you hate it, I won't even ask again." She's seriously the sweetest person ever, and I hate that she wants this so much. I roll my bottom lip in and glare at the screen. The lyrics scroll across the screen. I swallow and open my mouth to sing very softly and annoyingly monotone but on time. A gauge on the side of that screen turns green, marking the notes I hit, and it keeps glowing, seeding my confidence.

Portia bobs her head along, mouthing the words with me. I can't carry a tune, but the app doesn't seem to care about my pitch. It has some technology that senses the timing of the words.

I don't know how, but the gauge is overflowing by the time I am done with the first chorus. Maybe it's rigged or Portia has it on an easy setting to make me feel better, but since I'm doing well, I start the second verse. It's clearly the song choice that's helping, and I start to replace my shallow breaths with deep ones. When it's over, there's a pause on the screen. For a moment, I think it's jammed, but Portia leans over. "The app has to wait for your opponent to finish and compare scores."

Digital confetti falls over my screen and a giant "Congratulations!" flashes.

"I won?" My tired and rubbed-red eyes grow wide as a little bit of pride puffs up my chest. Christian always teases me there is no one on the planet who loves winning more than me, and I sort of agree. Even when I'm completely shattered, I still love winning.

The screen does some tally thing, and it flashes. "You've won a thousand diamonds."

"Look how many diamonds I won." I tap on the screen, watching them all pile up. "What do I do with them?"

"Since you start in the amateur level, nobody spends or wins money. So, this was just a way to make it fun. You can use the diamonds to level up your avatar and advance in levels, which will change the contestants you may challenge. If you make it to the pro level, you can win real prize money."

"Really?" My eyes are glued to the screen as these shiny diamonds just keep coming.

"Told you it was fun." Portia reaches over, taking her phone back from me, giving me the side-eye. "I'll text you a promo code for a free download."

I take a deep breath, about to tell her no thanks.

It's a silly game.

I don't have time for games.

However, upon second thought it was a mere three minutes of distraction that allowed my tears to dry. I'm not by any means healed, but I will take a distraction. "Thank you." I breathe a little easier as the flood of tears I was holding back earlier has seemed to lessen.

Christian pops his head out of his office. His front hair spike looking extra disgruntled. "Are you ready to get this show on the road?"

"Yeah." I stand, ready to walk out with him. "I'm ready to move on . . ."

Two

Arielle

We arrive in the heart of downtown Mapleton right around dinnertime and pull into the historic Harbor Inn and Lodge parking lot. I've visited plenty of small towns, but unlike most, where it's clear their better days are behind them with old infrastructure and deserted downtowns, Mapleton appears to be quite the opposite. People of all ages bustle in and out of downtown businesses from street corner to street corner, and everyone has a cheery smile on their face. I step out of the car and do a double take when I see I'm walking on an actual cobblestone covered street.

"This way." Christian motions toward a robin's-egg blue, two-story building. It's perfectly colored to match the pattern of all the other buildings surrounding it, resembling something out of a storybook.

Finding the bookstore sign right where it should be—above the door—I read it out loud, "The Bookshelf. Isn't that adorable!"

"You say adorable, but I say it looks like money." Christian rubs his hands together, the smirk on his face growing even wider. "I've been talking to the owner for weeks, and he's looking to expand coffee sales. He thinks franchising would be a great option—which I agree. I've pretty much got him sold on partnering with me for a Coffee Loft franchise."

We slow our steps, and I take in the large street window display full of paperback books. I can't help but think I've been here before, even though I know I haven't been. After pondering for a moment, I conclude the reason it looks familiar is it resembles the quaint little bookstores you see in Christmas movies.

Christian opens the wooden door, and we are hit with the scent of paper mixed with hints of vanilla and deep espresso. My nose perks at the scent cocktail. I'm not a huge reader, so the scent of new books doesn't excite me, but the coffee notes feel like home. My attention lands on an impossible-to-miss mahogany staircase that lines the wall, leading to an overhead loft filled with more books. We meander past it, like two lost people, toward the familiar sound of a milk steamer.

"Morning," a gentleman from behind the coffee bar calls as he snaps a plastic lid on the hot drink in front of him. He's tall, and with his head bent over the drink, his dark wavy hair flops almost over his eyes.

"You must be Graham." Christian steps forward, offering his steady hand over the bar. "I'm Christian Hanson."

"Oh, yes." Graham lifts his head, shaking his hair back and finding a hand towel, wiping his hands before he takes Christian's. "How do you do?"

"Excellent." Christian leaves on his business-neutral expression as he drops Graham's hand and turns to me. "This is my sister, Arielle."

Graham's gaze plants on me, and he extends his hand again. "Nice to meet you, Arielle." I shake his hand, and Graham nods to the barstools at the bar. "Welcome to my office. Have a seat. Can I make you a drink?"

"Thank you, but I've had plenty already." Christian waves off his gesture.

"No, thank you." I smile politely, and then stare past him to survey his bar. He has all his syrups on a bookshelf on the wall, which is cute since it's a bookstore. It wouldn't be my first choice to put the coffee bar way in the back of the store, but he has it decorated well, with lots of coffee pun signs and colored mugs hanging on the wall.

"I'm glad you made it over here." Graham takes the coffee he had just prepared and lifts the cup to his mouth, sipping out of it. "I've been reading about Coffee Loft for months, and I'm a huge fan of what they're doing."

"Same. Once I started looking into their franchise, I knew it was perfect for me. I'm certain you'll love it too. The buy-in is lower than most other coffee franchises." Christian holds up a finger to make his point and continues to add a finger with each point he counts off. "Their yearly fees are lower. They have better quality products, and the opportunity is endless, as there is no saturation."

"It sounds perfect for my situation. My wife and I are about to have a baby." Graham's happy life slams me back inside my head, where I can't help but feel a sting of sadness. Not that he's married—well, he is handsome with dark-blue eyes set behind thick lashes—but I had been doing okay. It had been at least an hour since I thought about my heartbreak. Hearing him achieve a milestone reminds me I recently got sent all the way back to the bench and am starting all over again. Again, the tears bud in the backs of my eyes, and I struggle to hold them back. I hate that it makes me sad to hear someone else is happy, but I desperately want that to be me.

"Weekends are our busiest days," Graham continues. "My wife and teenage daughter usually come to help. That way, there's always someone at the bookstore checkout and the coffee bar. With Elinora having the baby, she needs to be home more, and Hadley's going to be hopefully off to college after this year. It's made me consider my options, where I don't have to rely on them so much. I'm so busy with the bookstore, I would love to bring in a partner to manage the coffee bar. I think if it's done well, I'd make the same money, but with half the hassle."

"I hear what you're saying." Christian rubs his chin, and I can literally see dollar signs bling in his eyes. "That's right up my alley. I have one shop on Long Island, and I've done a lot to turn it around. I would love another location, but I can't be in two places at once. I love the idea that we'd be partners. You could be here to monitor it, but essentially, I'd manage it, train, and hire the staff. I think it would work well." Christian turns on his heel, scanning the store again. It's quaint compared to his huge Long Island location, but that dollar-sign gleam in the corner of his eye tells me he's already sold. "I love your store. It's so cozy in here, and Mapleton seems like a great little town," he adds, buttering up Graham even more.

"It's great. I moved here in my early twenties. Later, I moved away for what I thought were better career opportunities, but this always felt like home. So, after I got married, we came back, and we love it." Graham nods to the door, not unwelcoming, but excitement shines through his smile. "Why don't you spend some time downtown and get to know the area? I've already signed the contracts you sent over, but I don't want you to have any buyer's remorse. Even though I'm certain you won't. If everything checks out, I think tomorrow morning we can officially make this transition."

"That sounds like an excellent idea." Christian rocks back on his heels, surveying the place one more time. I've seen that glazed over expression before. I bet he's already envisioning himself carrying loads of money to the bank. I shake my head, rather amused. Christian is good for a distraction from my miserable life. It has been at least another minute since the last time I thought about Tom . . .

I'm getting better.

I think.

Except for this rock that I have in my gut that's so heavy, it makes it hard to pretend I'm normal. I try my best to ignore it and continue forward out the door with Christian into the crisp winter air. We amble back down the block to the lodge.

As soon as we pass through the sliding front doors, we are met with the most gorgeous mountain lodge décor. An enormous stone fireplace fills the far wall, and a roaring fire crackles, bringing warmth to the entire room. Knotty pine beams frame out the high angled ceiling, and I instantly feel welcome. My shoulders fall, releasing tension, and I'm suddenly ready to relax.

We check into our room and walk down the hall, both of us checking our phones for messages. Christian's busy texting Portia—those two are so cute—they never stop talking. The rock in my gut swells when I see I have no messages.

Not that I want to hear from Tom.

However, there's an obvious void in my life that is going to take some time to fill. It's like I have a nervous jitter now as I wonder what I should be doing with my time, now that I shouldn't be thinking about Tom.

Christian swipes his key card to unlock the door to our room and winces. "I forgot to pack underwear."

I sputter out laughing. "Don't think you're going to be sitting next to me."

He extends his arm, holding the door open for me to pass through. "Nah, I saw there was a general store right down the block. You make yourself at home. I'll run over there before it closes."

I roll my suitcase forward, finding the perfect spot to park it in the closet. "Can you pick up something to eat too?"

His unruly brows stoop down as his gaze bounces around my face, and he asks in a kind voice, "You don't want to go out for dinner?"

Tugging one side of my lips into a lopsided grin, I force a positive expression. "I don't care to go out. Takeout sounds so much better." His gaze hangs on me, and I rush out, "It's not about Tom."

After a long beat of silence, he finally replies, "Sure, I can find some burgers or something."

The way he looks at me with his eyes so full of empathy makes tears prick the backs of my eyes, and I get choked up. The only thing I can force out is, "Thank you."

"Sure thing, El." He backs out of the room, softly closing the door behind him, and I'm left alone.

The rock in my gut balloons, feeling ten times heavier, and I grab my stomach to brace it. I can't hold it in for another second. Tears rapidly fall down my face, and I swipe them away as I scurry to the bathroom for a tissue. I've never been a huge crier, but this isn't a normal breakup. I thought Tom and I were going to be married. I quit college so I could be closer to him. I was so dumb for thinking that was a good idea. Now I have no job skills, and the only job I could get was cleaning. I screwed up my life and all I got in return is a broken heart.

I ugly cry, letting my shoulders shake, and I blow my nose into a tissue. I let it all out before Christian gets back, because he won't tolerate me crying over Tom. After all my sobs are out, I blow my nose one more time and toss my tissue into the trash. I take a deep breath, clearing my head of all things Tom, and I mentally draw a line to be done crying. I need to clean up before Christian gets back. I splash water on my face, drag my feet back to the bedroom, and pick up my phone. My throat instantly dries when I see an unread text message.

No, not Tom.

It's the code for the karaoke app that Portia told me she'd send me. A frown of forlornity tugs on my lips.

I will not sing karaoke.

Especially not here in a hotel room.

Portia has the wildest ideas.

I mean, if that's what she likes to do, then more power to her. Shaking my head, I let my fingers hover over the code as I'm ready to delete it. My gaze floats back to the door.

The room is empty.

No one would hear me.

It distracted me last time.

Right on cue, the rock in my gut swells, threatening to spring more tears.

I just cleaned up from ugly crying. I can't cry like that again.

I need a distraction.

At least until Christian gets back.

My fingers tremble as the tears travel up from the rock in my gut, and I panic and click on the code.

Anything is better than crying.

THREE

Stallone Hart

My eyelids shoot open, darkness is all around me, the wind howling so loudly it sounds like a freight train is barreling through my front door. I glance at the alarm clock on my bedside table and groan. 3:00 a.m.

Always, I'm up at this hour, as my life seems to be stuck on autopilot.

On this unordinary day in the middle of a not-special week, the house shutters and the evergreen branches scrape at my bedroom window, but I'm not scared. I've heard worse. It does, however, prick at my mind, telling me I won't be going to work. A knot swells in my throat, and I swallow to force it down, but it stays. The knot doesn't care about the money, as I have more of that than I'd ever dreamed of.

It's a knot of avoidance.

And it's a real jerk, reminding me to keep busy so I don't remember *her.*

I swing my legs over the edge of the bed, force my tired body to my feet, on the hunt for a glass of cold water to soothe my throat. It's been ages since I slept through the night, and getting up way before the first light of dawn is my pattern. I shuffle my feet forward until my hand finds the cool stainless-steel handle on the fridge. I grab a bottle of water and down most of it before I pivot and turn on my coffeepot. It gurgles to life while I lean over the kitchen sink to peer out the window into the night sky.

The light I always leave on above my front porch for security reveals a blanket of fluffy snow has already accumulated in my yard, and all the branches on my pine trees are bowing down from the weight. Sighing, I turn away. The moisture isn't a bad thing. It's the fact the rural backcountry roads have nearly washed-out with mudslides, making it impossible for my oversized trucks to haul logs to the mill. We've been piling up everything we chop until the roads dry out. This weather is going to turn the mudslides into ice, which is so much worse.

This means another few days—at best—until I can move wood.

I run my hand through my hair, pretending it's pain in my head and not my heart that keeps me up. Right as I'm about to let out a defeated sigh, Lucky stirs awake from his spot by the front door and walks over, greeting me with his tail wagging. Lucky is a stray I found roaming these hills. He got his name after he narrowly missed getting slammed by a tree. I used to call him Lucky Nine Lives, but he has far surpassed nine lives in the two years he's been my logging partner.

He's also gotten used to my predawn rising, and he's ready to go for our walk. "Just a moment, boy." I pat his head before filling a travel mug with black coffee. I always take my coffee to go, as it keeps me warm on our walks. "Let me get dressed, and we'll be on our way."

I head to the door, where all my outer clothes are neatly hung on hooks, and I slip on my thickest lined flannel shirt and cover it with a pair of coveralls. I slide my feet into a pair of snow boots and tug a thick beanie over my head. The front door isn't even cracked before Lucky pushes his nose out, leading the way.

The frigid air slams into the inside of my lungs, pulling me out of any remnants of slumber I was holding on to. It's an odd sensation to welcome the sting of the wind, because at least for the moment, I can blame my pain on something temporal. I take a deep inhale, as there is nothing better than the fresh mountain breeze, and start off on our regular morning walking trail with Lucky running all around me in search of fresh scents.

When we coast around the bend in the road, I toss a look over at my little brother's cabin. It's only a few hundred yards from where Ryson and I grew up, in a cabin of humble beginnings. Ryson's younger by five years and completely my opposite. He's socially outgoing and can barely stay out of trouble, except for the fact that he's a smooth talker. Me, being the more introverted, reliable brother always trying to talk sense into him.

All the windows in Ryson's cabin are dark—as they should be for this time of the morning. I can't help but envy his ability to sleep. He doesn't have the stress I have running a company. He drives a truck for me, except for when he can't, like now. Then he watches TV. I sigh heavily and carry on the path as it narrows and winds around another bend—this one is my favorite one of all. The point that overlooks the entire city of Mapleton.

It's the perfect town, in my opinion. Small enough that you know everyone by name, but large enough you have the local businesses you need for a proper community. Quaint cobblestone streets are lined with old-fashioned streetlamps, and I never get tired of looking at the glow they create down below. It's like tiny stars at the bottom of a valley that watch over the people while they sleep.

A few wispy snowflakes flutter to the ground, as if they are tasked with the job of adding the finishing touches on the already blanketed streets. It all appears magical from up here, and I never tire of seeing—wait a second . . .

My brows bend together as the streetlamps pulse off and on twice in unison before finally settling into the darkness, and the little town at the bottom of the mountain almost disappears.

I slow my steps, easing closer to the edge of the trail and wait for the lamps to turn back on. Several long beats pass, but all the lamps remain dark. Clearly, the town has lost power. More than likely some power lines have fallen under the weight of this dense snow. My cabin is powered by propane, so it won't affect me, but if they don't fix the power lines soon, people will get awfully cold fast.

My gaze slides back down. I still can't see even a spark, but I know how to help them. I have so many logs piled up; it would be nothing for me to take a load to town for firewood. I slide my fingers into my mouth, whistling through them. "Come on, Lucky. Time to go."

His tongue hangs low, and his tail sweeps back and forth. He's as happy as a clam on a beach, fully unaware that people are about to freeze from this power outage. His smile is contagious, erasing at least some of my heartsick- ness. I stride next to him; glad I have a companion.

Lucky pushes his snout into my leg as he follows on my heels. I pat his head, chuckling to myself.

If only a pat on my head could make me that happy.

Four

Arielle

I wiggle my toes and pull the scratchy comforter tighter around my neck, but it does nothing to warm me. "Christian," I hiss over the narrow aisle between our queen beds. "Did you turn the air conditioner on?" It's pitch dark in the hotel room, but I angle my gaze toward Christian's heavy breathing.

When he doesn't reply because he's still sound asleep, I take my spare pillow and whip it toward him, the way a sister should smack her annoying big brother. "Christian," I say, raising my voice as my eyes slowly adjust to the darkness.

"Whoa, what?" He startles awake.

"Did you turn the air on?" I wrap my blanket even tighter around me, but shivers erupt from my extremities.

It's absolutely freezing, and these thin hotel blankets don't hold any warmth.

"Why, yes, I keep the air on full blast in January in New England because I love to bleed money." He pauses for a beat before adding, "The clock isn't glowing. I would guess the power went out."

"Ah, great," I mumble under my breath and reach for my phone, which I had set on the nightstand. I click the power button, relieved to see a tiny flash of light and use it to guide me to my suitcase for a sweatshirt. "I didn't pack for a power outage." I shiver as I also find my winter beanie, and yank it on, covering the bottoms of my ears. I don't stop dressing until after I've slipped on my down winter coat—it's that cold in here.

"I'm sure it will be on shortly," Christian speaks through a yawn.

My phone confirms it's almost time to start the day. "It's after six. The sun should come up soon. That might help warm things up a little." I hustle back to my bed, crawl under the blankets, and stare toward the window.

"You should try having high blood pressure like me. Then you'll never be bothered by the cold." Christian's grumble is muffled by the pillow he's pulled over his head to more than likely tune me out.

"Wait a second." My head springs back from an image that flashes in my brain. "Do you remember when we checked into the lodge last night? The lobby had that huge stone fireplace. Do you think we should sit downstairs until the power comes back on?"

Christian's sleepy grumble is barely audible. "I mean, it doesn't make sense to just lie in bed to relax."

"Right." I ignore his sarcasm and spring to my feet. "It's too cold in here, even under the blankets. They had those big leather couches downstairs. It's perfect." I'm already slipping on my Uggs when I toss a glance over my shoulder. He hasn't moved from his spot in bed. "Let's hurry before someone else gets the same idea and takes our spot." I yank on the doorknob and prompt the door open with my foot. "Last one down has to buy the other person breakfast."

"No power means nobody will get breakfast." Christian drops one foot to the carpet and does a falling motion to get out of bed. It's ungraceful and seems a bit harsh, but Christian has a dramatic way of doing most things. He whisks his phone off the nightstand and shuffles his feet forward, mumbling through another yawn, "Besides, I need to get dressed." He takes a minute to swap his shorts for pants, slips on a jacket, and then loafers before he stares at me for the first time this morning. "Happy now?" he grumbles.

"Not until we get our spot." I rush him out the door. We follow the dark hall, guided only by the light on my cell phone, as it seems the rest of the hotel customers are still asleep. It might be my optimistic imagination, but I feel the temperature increase as we get closer to the lobby.

"I guess the interstate is closed." Christian reads a notification on his phone. "We won't be going home today."

I'm about to let out a groan but the lobby comes into view and the permeating warmth muffles my annoyance. The massive stone fireplace doesn't disappoint with a soft glowing fire to welcome me. I smile slyly at the desk attendant as I beeline to the couch in front of the fireplace. "Our room is so cold, I couldn't sleep," I say and plop down, scooting my body all the way to the armrest closest to the flame.

"The power has been out for several hours already," he reports in a monotone voice. "The forecast said it's just a pause in the snow, as it's supposed to dump more later this morning."

"Oh, look. That's Graham from The Bookshelf going in to work." Christian uses his index finger to point out the window while he scratches his belly with his other hand. Happy to not watch him scratch, I willingly follow his gesture.

Sure enough, Graham's unlocking the bookstore. "I guess this city never shuts down."

"I guess not." Christian jerks his head to the exit as his feet move toward it. "We might as well head over too and start our first day."

"Can you hear yourself talking right now?" I stumble to my feet, hating to leave the warm haze from the fire. "You are obsessed with money." I wave my hand over his body. "You haven't even showered for the day, nor have I."

"I'm not going to shower without hot water. Plus, nobody cares how I'm dressed." His face is stern, focused, telling me there's no use in protesting. Christian is that kind of guy who can never sit still, especially if he's anxious about something. It's his turn to lead, and out the door we go. I'm grateful the sun is starting to peek over the mountain range, but still unimpressed by the frosty air that nips at my extremities. I tug on my coat, both concealing my warmth and my nightshirt.

"Morning, Graham!" Christian calls out across the road as I struggle to keep pace with Christian's perky steps. We race right to Graham like we're stalkers. "Lovely day, isn't it?"

Graham's gaze finds us, and he immediately responds to Christian's sarcasm with a chuckle. "Right. So nice out."

"I think the whole town is out of power." I steel my face to the ground. Christian is so embarrassing sometimes as he states the most obvious things.

"We lost power at our house a few hours ago, but the store has a generator." Graham turns his key, releasing the door. He yanks it open with one smooth motion and jerks his head in an inviting nod. "Come on in. I'll see if I can make some coffee."

Graham switches the closed sign to open and heads toward the back, disappearing through a door that appears to lead to another staircase. After a few moments, the lights flicker on, and the fan of the furnace hums, bringing a promise of incoming warmth. I almost cheer. It's funny how you never think of electricity until you've lost it, but I couldn't be happier to see artificial light.

When Graham reappears, he has a full smile on his face and heads behind the coffee bar, flicking on the drip coffeepot and espresso machine. "There's a tiny apartment upstairs that I used to live in. Before I lived there, the old lady who owned this store before me lived in it, and she had to be on oxygen when she was older. They had that generator installed for emergencies, but it comes in handy."

"I bet." Christian takes long strides toward the coffee bar and straddles a barstool like he already owns the place. His flashing dollar signs return to his pupils. "I love what you've done here. I can't wait to see this place grow even more."

"Yeah, like I said before, if it wasn't for the fact my wife and I are expecting a baby, I'd keep plugging along. However, I learned the hard way with my daughter that I need to be home more, and running a bookstore is plenty enough on its own." Graham casually takes his phone out of his pocket, and starts setting it on the counter, when his gaze flicks to it momentarily, and his eyebrows practically shoot to the ceiling. "Oh, my!"

"Everything okay?" Christian arches his chin, trying to peek at the phone in the most not-nonchalant manner.

"Ah, not sure." Graham is rapidly texting, his eyes locked on his phone. "My wife's water broke, but it's too early for the baby." His gaze cuts to Christian. "I've got to go."

The front door jingles open, and a couple meanders in. "Guys, we're closed," Graham calls out while he digs in his pocket and pulls out a set of keys. He takes several steps toward the exit. "I need to leave."

"Oh, I saw the lights on, and thought it was a place we could keep warm," the man says while rubbing his bright pink hands together. "Our apartment is out of heat."

"I was going to open." Graham's words rush faster as he continues to the front and switches the open sign back to closed. "But that was before I found out my wife is in labor, and now I need to go."

"Oh, we're sorry," the woman says while the small smile she had been wearing noticeably plummets when she pivots to return outside.

I know how she feels.

The wind is howling, the snow is blowing, and I'm getting the shivers just thinking about going outside. I don't want to go back to our freezing hotel room. "Ah, maybe you don't have to leave." My voice cracks and I clear my throat, tossing a look at Graham. "I can make them a coffee and give them a place to sit until they warm up a little."

"I don't know about that." Graham's expression pulls into a wince. "It seems like a big ask to leave you guys here. I really think we need to just lock up."

"Well," Christian speaks matter-of-factly, "Today is our day to transition everything, so really the coffee bar is mine, right? It really makes sense for us to stay. We can just tell everyone the bookstore is closed but we are here."

Graham's wince deepens as his gaze bounces from me to Christian and back to the couple. The couple's smiles droop even more as they back away from the counter. "It's just coffee, and we can handle it," I say. "Christian and I both know our way around a coffee bar, and we have nothing else to do."

Graham's silent but he turns to Christian, who doesn't disappoint, piping up again, "It'll give me a chance to get to know the customers."

Graham's gaze bounces from the couple to Christian, and then his phone rings. He yanks it out of his pocket. "Hello?" His inflections are strained as he lowers his voice, but it doesn't conceal the conversation that his wife's waiting for him. Christian steps forward, waving Graham out the door. "Just go. You have my number. Call when you know she's safe. I'll help these people." Graham takes a moment to look around the shop again, before giving a deep shrug, and eventually nods an agreement with his phone still glued to his ear.

I turn on my heel and head to the coffee bar. "What can I start for you?" I ask the couple.

They step forward. The guy, who is dressed in very nice business attire, says, "Just hot coffee would be great."

"I can handle that." I easily find the cups and pivot to fill them, but the coffeepot that Graham had switched on seems to have been backed up. There's hot water in the pot, but no coffee. I open the back of the machine and check for grounds. They are there. I flip the switch off and then on, but it only makes a dying noise. Pursing my lips, I study it. I can't see any switches I'm missing.

Maybe Graham has it on a rinse cycle?

There must be a switch or something I need to use to get it out of hot water mode that I don't know. Under my breath, I hiss at Christian, who's watching me do all the labor. "Can you look at this?"

He takes long strides over and stands in front of it with his hands on his hips. "I'm looking."

Sometimes I just don't have the patience for his humor, and I sigh and turn back to the couple. Now I understand Graham's hesitation for leaving us here. Apparently, there's a trick to his coffeepot that isn't obvious. I'm not calling him while he's already so stressed out. "New plan," I say slowly, "I have hot water but no coffee. How about some tea?"

"Yeah, that sounds fine," they both quickly agree, and the woman points to the jars directly behind me. "That breakfast blend looks great."

"Deal." I ready their teas, and I check the menu for the price and turn to the tablet on the counter. Thankfully, it has full charge, and it's pretty much the same point-of-sale system Christian uses at the Coffee Loft, and I'm able to ring them up.

When they leave, Christian's beaming at me. "You just love getting us into these things, don't you?"

"Me?" I jerk my thumb to my chest defensively. "You're the one who made us come over here this morning."

"I wanted to get things swapped over to Coffee Loft. I didn't volunteer to run the place with no training. I know nothing about these machines, and they look so vintage compared to what I'm used to. I had planned to shut the place down as soon as I get the key to remodel."

"How hard can it be?" I gesture toward the espresso machine behind me. "It's not half as complicated as the Coffee Loft fancy stuff." By now the heat has returned to the room, and I'm getting used to feeling my fingers. I don't want to go outside or back to the hotel where there's no heat. "If you don't want to figure it out, then don't. I'm not going back to that hotel. If I'm going to stay here, the least I can do is give people a warm drink."

"I guess," he mutters as he joins me behind the counter. "I might as well start doing inventory." His eyes pace the bookshelf of syrups. "I need to run back to the hotel to grab my laptop—"

The door pulls open, bringing in a powerful gust of wind, and a swirl of glittering snow, followed by the biggest, burliest man I've ever seen. His shoulders are so broad they fill the doorway, and his face is covered in a thick dark beard, the very tips of his whiskers frosted with snowflakes. He seemingly knows his way around the place as he crosses the bookstore and heads straight toward me.

"Morning." His voice is gruff, but not unfriendly as he catches me staring. "Some weather we have here, huh?"

"R-Right." I stammer and close my mouth before I catch the logo on his shirt, *Hart Logging,* and I ask the most obvious question just to make small talk, "Are you a logger?"

"When I can get to work." There's a gleam in the corner of his eye that is so warm I fight the urge to stare at him. He gestures forward. "I'm also a coffee addict, and I saw the lights were on."

It's easy to return his smile, but I'm not sure why my face is suddenly feeling so much warmer. "Yeah, I'm happy to help you."

He cuts his gaze back to the menu. "I'll take a large black coffee."

I grab the cup and turn toward the coffeepot, and a frown pulls on my lips. The pot still only has water. I push the on button again. From the noise it's making, I doubt it will work. "Ah, my coffeepot is broken today." I pull up one side of my lips into a lopsided grin. "I'm actually not really working here, as I'm just filling in. So, I hate to mess with it and break it more, but I have hot water. I can make any tea."

"Tea?" he echoes as if I've said a curse word.

"Sorry." I smile politely and quickly motion to the assortment of jars behind me, all filled with tea leaves. "I always love a good black tea, and I can add milk and some vanilla flavor."

His bushy eyebrows bend down, but he grunts. "If that's all you have, I guess."

I get busy steeping his tea leaves in hot water, but I can feel his stony stare on me, which pricks my nerves a bit. I ask another question to keep the conversation going. "So, what are you up to today in this blizzard?"

"I'm in the park with firewood. If you know anyone who needs any, send them my way."

"I'm new to town." I add the lid to his cup and place it on the bar in front of him. "I haven't met many people yet."

My gaze snags on his hands when he passes me his debit card. With raw callous scabs covering the tops of his palms, his whole hand is easily the width of two of mine. My gaze trails down his arms, and I struggle to not let my jaw hit the floor. His arms are so round, they are practically the size of Tom's whole scrawny body. My cheeks warm at the comparison, and I force my gaze back to his face. "Just two dollars," I say and swipe his card through the Square before I hand it back.

Our gazes linger on one another as we exchange good-byes, and the lumberjack exits the building, leaving a trail of the whole evergreen forest behind. I've never seen a man like that before, and he's left me with a strong curiosity.

"Don't even think about it." Christian's warning cuts into my thoughts like nails on a chalkboard.

"What?" I cut a glance back at him, defensiveness building in my chest. "What are you talking about?"

"I saw the way you were drooling over him." He chuckles, shaking his head. "The last thing you need is a big old mountain man to break your heart while we're here."

"Who said anything about romance?" I snap back, hating how Christian jumps to conclusions. I never thought for a single moment about him breaking my heart.

I've sworn off men.

I was simply admiring his scent.

And his beard.

And his big strong hands.

And his enormous arms.

And his kind eyes.

Yeah, he has an awful lot of good qualities to think about. I pinch my lips together, holding back a secret smile. Out of my peripheral vision, I catch the lumberjack's backside in front of the big storefront window as he crosses the street.

He certainly is easy to look at.

And an excellent distraction from the fact I've sworn off dating forever.

"All right." Christian's stance straightens toward the door. "Enough stalling. I'm going to run to the hotel, grab my laptop, and see if they can extend our room for another night since the roads are closed. Is there anything you need me to grab for you?"

I survey the store, and the only people in here are the first couple. It's pretty uneventful. "I should be fine."

He throws up his palm as he marches forward. "Be back in a bit."

I watch him leave and then because I no longer have an excuse to avoid it, I pull out my phone and text my dad

Me: Hey, Dad, I'm not going to be in for another day or two. Christian and I ended up getting snowed in.

Dots indicating he's typing show on my screen for a long time, which is weird because my dad hates texting, and he usually only types one or two words. The amount of time it shows him typing makes me think that he's going to lecture me about something.

Dad: Everything else okay?

My top teeth crash down on my bottom lip, as I reread his text and wonder if he suspects something else is up.

Had he heard the rumors about Tom? I can't even begin to think about how I'm going to explain that whole thing to him.

Me: Yeah, it's fine. Just helping at the coffee shop today.

I drop my phone onto the counter before I'm tempted to add anything else. Now determined to get my mind on other things, I turn back to the coffee bar with my eyes on the broken coffeepot. *There must be a button or something I'm missing.* Running my hand all along the base, I can't find anything that even resembles a button or a switch. I grab the plug out of the wall and plug it back into a different outlet. Still nothing. A cool breeze comes in from behind me, alerting me to the front door being open, and I toss a glance in that direction.

It's just Christian.

"Back already?" I push the coffeepot back to its original spot and step away from it.

"Yeah." He's breathing heavy, most likely from running, and he plops his backpack on the table near the front window before he takes a moment to brush the fresh powder snow off the bottoms of his pant legs. "It's really coming down."

"I figured." I slowly stride to the front of the store and peek out the large front window. There's so much frost accumulated on the glass, it's hard to see except for a few bare spots right in the center. "Did you notice if anything else is open? I'd love to see if I can find a coffeepot."

"Nah, there really isn't a point since Coffee Loft has its own brand. Just wait until we get our franchise one. That's better than anything you'll find at the store." Christian unzips his bag, pulls out a thick black binder, and sets it on the table in front of him.

I turn my gaze back out and study the town. Mounds of snow are piled up on the sidewalks, making some places nearly impossible to walk. The streets have yet to be plowed, and there's just a single lane of tracks blazed through the snow by the trucks that risked travel. Town is essentially deserted except for in the center of town where there is a park and a single truck pulled over with firewood in the back.

That must be that man who was just here...

"What are you looking at?" Christian holds his gaze on me, as if I'm accountable to him.

"Just the snow everywhere." I shove my hands in my pockets and move away from the window, sneaking another peek at the truck before I turn completely away. "You know, since you're back, I might step out for some fresh air."

"Did you already forget it's freezing out?" Arching his chin, his gaze slams to the window like he's inspecting the outside for something he suspects he missed. His smile grows flimsy when his eyes roam over on the lone truck. "El..."

My lips curl against my will, and I move toward the door before Christian has more time to solve this riddle. I push the door open and step out, calling back, "Just grabbing some fresh air . . ."

I turn toward the park, and add under my breath and only for me, "And a better view."

FIVE

Stallone

"Oh, thank you so much, Stallone," Mrs. Beasily, the old lady who owns the laundromat, clenches her patent leather coin purse in front of her and watches as I load up two bundles of firewood in the trunk of her old red Buick. I've already given out half my load of wood today. If my calculations are correct, I should be able to head home within the hour.

"It's my pleasure." Her trunk smells like dog food, and I'm grateful when I get to shut it, and turn to head into my truck. I left it running with the heater cranked, and it's comfortable.

Her frail, bony fingers find my forearm, causing me to pause on my heel. "What do I owe you?"

"Not a thing." I shake my head, adding a please-to-serve-you smile to my face. "It's my pleasure. I just hope you stay warm."

"Oh, goodness." She squeezes my arm tighter, and I fight the urge to wince as I've never been much of a person who enjoys people in my space. "How about I bake you a potato pie once the power comes on?"

"I didn't know potato had a pie." One of my brows hikes above the other into a quizzical expression. Nothing about that word combination sounds appealing. She's still got hold of my arm, and I frankly don't care to argue if it extends this encounter. "Sure, but only if you go home now, because it's too cold for you to stand out here."

Her eyes spring wide for a moment, but she bows her head a bit and says, "All right. I'll see you soon."

"Stay warm." I toss a silent wave up, as snow crunching from nearby footsteps draws my attention to turn the opposite direction and I freeze. The woman I had just spoken to earlier at the coffee shop is headed this way. Her hood is pulled up tight around her head, adding a little extra fluff of fur trim around her face, but that doesn't take away from her gorgeous icy-blue eyes. I wave at her, curious about what she's doing. She said she didn't need any wood, and it's way too cold out here to just stand around. She waves back and when she smiles, her smile is mischievous and focuses right at me. "Did you change your mind about needing some firewood?"

She shields her face from the blowing snow. "No, I don't need any. I was just going to stop over—"

"Stall*ooone*!" A shrill noise that frequents my nightmares cuts through the air, stealing both of our attentions. My eyelids crash down, and I know who it is before I ever complete my blink.

Nora Worley.

The single most annoying woman I've ever laid eyes on. She can never say a smooth Stallone. It was always crooning out, Sta*looooone,* drawing it out like a game show host who's being choked. I grunt and brush my hand over my whiskers, turning enough to see her walking this way. "Stallooone Hart," she croons out again, her hips swaying in an exaggerated way until she stops a few feet from me and the coffeehouse lady.

"Did you need some wood?" I ask with a straight face. No time is ever a good time to have to see her, but this is the worst timing, because I really was interested in talking to the coffee shop lady. I flicker my gaze back to her, hoping she doesn't walk off. She's biting her bottom lip—which in my humble analysis—doesn't look like a good thing.

"No wood." Nora's voice is unnaturally loud like she's trying to speak over a crowd that isn't here. "I need you to call me back for once."

"You called?" I blink, terrified she might have my phone number. I never gave her that, and if by chance I had given her my number, I'll change it.

"No, I didn't call. It's just proper manners to call people after *a date*." Her T is extra enunciated, making it sound even more terrifying.

"Date?" I choke out an echo, as I have no idea what she's talking about. I haven't been on a date in over a year, and I certainly would never go on a date with her.

Her lips pinch together momentarily before she says, "Remember, two nights ago, we had drinks?"

What are you even talking about?

Coffeehouse girl starts to slide her feet, backing away, and I feel the strained expression on my face that wants to ask her to stay, but I have no idea where this conversation is going. *Nora is clearly delusional!*

She may say something I don't want anyone to hear. Instead of calling out for her to stay, I flash my palm to her and say, "Stay warm." She gives me a mellow smile and turns to trudge back to the coffee shop. The sight of her leaving sends a ping of disappointment right to my gut. My annoyance at Nora's presence quadruples, and I blurt back, "I didn't go out with you. I grabbed a to-go dinner from The Grove and went home."

"Right." She nods as if I'm a small child not understanding instructions. "Remember we sat together at the bar and had drinks, and we laughed. It was such a nice time."

I jab my hand through my hair, resisting the urge to yell at this woman. I ordered a drink while I waited for my food, and she plopped down next to me and talked about her hair salon business the whole time.

I wasn't listening.

Maybe I'm good at pretending.

She thought that was a date?

I almost vomit in my mouth. "That wasn't a date, Nora. You can't go around saying it was."

She perks an over-tweezed eyebrow at me. "You hugged me extra long when we left."

"I stood up to leave, and you basically threw your arms around my neck. What was I supposed to do?" I tried to forget about it because it had to be the most cringe moment of my year, and having to flesh this out now with Nora is making my blood pressure soar. I know when to pick my arguments, and this isn't one I want. "Look, I'm done here for now." I pivot and slam the tailgate shut and don't offer another word when I climb in my truck.

By now, coffeehouse lady is all the way back to the coffee shop. I see her open the door and disappear inside. I so badly want to make Nora disappear too. I don't have the patience for pleasantries or pretending that she isn't completely nuts. She's been trying to get with me for years, and I've always been as much of a gentleman about it as I could stand, but this is too much.

Of all the things to have happened, Nora is going around telling people we went on a date. What next?

This is why I stay away from town and people in general. I rant in my head as I crank my truck and steer back to my house, feeling as if I just dodged a bullet. All the good women are taken and I'm not desperate enough to deal with a nut.

Another day on autopilot. I wake before dawn and reach across my bed, finding it cold and empty. I blink, wishing my view would change.

It never does.

It's a feeling of being lost in your own home, in my own bed. I'm supposed to be living through my first year of marriage right now, not in this constant state of heartache. The quicker I get out of bed, the sooner I can breathe.

Today, I walk straight to the front door—eager for all the distractions—and whip it open. My head jolts back at the chill, and my eyes are met with more snow. It's frozen hard, which means the roads will be too. It's a tad risky to take the semi out, but the news reported Mapleton had their power restored last night. I'm not needed in town today, and I can't sit around all day and let my mind wander. I power through the motions to get ready with my usual clothes and coffee.

Whistling, I summon Lucky, and he eagerly runs to my truck and jumps in, and we putter down the winding roads, stopping at Ryson's cabin and honking the horn until he manifests in his Hart Logging flannel shirt and cargo pants—coffee mug in hand. We Hart brothers are serious about our coffee.

"Did you get enough sleep there, Lazy?" I tease, and Lucky makes his way over to sit on his lap. Lucky clearly isn't a lap dog as he weighs over seventy pounds, but nobody could ever convince him otherwise. He's also so tall, he has to duck his head to fit, but he doesn't whimper a complaint.

"There wasn't much else to do but sleep." Ryson lifts his mug to his lips, sipping. "How are the roads?"

"Slick and terrible," I grumble as I shift the truck back into gear and pull out carefully to avoid spinning out.

"Perfect." His easy grin fills his face, and he lets out a sarcastic snicker. "That's exactly how I like them."

The thing about being a logger is it's the perfect job for introverted people like me. I never have to say much. I turn up the tunes on the radio and drive on. Me, thinking about the woman I should be over. Ryson, more than likely wondering what beer combo goes best with wings. And then there's Lucky, who just chills and gets his back scratched.

As I pass the lumber mill, my gaze scans over the yard filled to the brim with logs. There's not a single truck lined up to drop off logs or move any out. I simply turn my head away. Apparently, that invites Ryson to talk.

"Did you hear Nora Worley is back in town?" It's been nearly a half hour of silence, and that's how he breaks it?

The last thing I need to talk about is Nora Worley. I'd sooner drive this truck right over the edge of the mountain than ever hear her name again. "No thanks."

Ryson's head locks forward on the road. "It's time you start living again. You've grieved over Lindsey long enough. She's not worth it."

I click my tongue on the roof of my mouth, holding back all the things I dare not say. Trust me, I think about it every day. Every day I feel the same. Dating is the last thing I'd ever want to do again. It's right up there with hearing from Nora again. Maybe I'm a fool or just too fragile, but I have to believe if I'm meant to love again, the very thought of it won't feel like my heart is being ripped out of my chest.   .

We fall into a stony silence until I pull into our worksite and back a trailer right up to the timber crane. With logs already piled up, it's an easy switch for Ryson to jump into the semi. "You need to go to the mill in Carson County," I say, even though I'm sure he saw our mill was closed. It doesn't really make sense for him to drive the extra hundred miles, as the gas bill cuts into our profits, but I need a reason to be busy.

I'm eager to be alone and hop into the crane, which fires up easily, despite the cold temps. We settle into an easy grind, filling his trailer in no time. It's monotonous work that leaves plenty of time for thinking. Most days I wear earbuds with upbeat music to keep my mind off Lindsey but today, something odd happens.

I think about yesterday.

I had left the bookstore holding a warm cup of the sweetest smelling tea I'd ever smelled. Course, I know nothing about tea except for that horrid stuff my mom used to force down my throat when I was a young child with a chest cold.

That tea yesterday was so different. When I tipped that cup up, and the warm, creamy liquid hit my tongue, my taste buds sprang wide awake, wanting even more. I could definitely go for another one of those. More than that, I think about the woman who made the tea. She seemed so eager to help me, despite her machine being broken. She had this sweet smile that lit up the entire room, even though she was quite small and compact for a chick.

Petite—I think is the proper word.

But she didn't give off the air of being a helpless damsel. She had a gleam in her eyes that told me she prefers to be sweet, but she wasn't afraid to be sassy. Although, she is as attractive as any model you'd see in a magazine, I spared a second glance because I am not looking for anything, especially not some girl who thinks tea is an adequate substitute for coffee. The nerve.

Ryson waves at me, indicating his trailer is full. I back up, and he pulls his semi out of the yard. I'm not ready to go home, and the sun is still peeking out behind the clouds. I might as well work while I'm here. I fill up two more trailers without hardly trying. Right as I'm leaving the yard, Ryson texts me.

Ryson: The lumber mill approved my delivery. They said they can take more tomorrow.

Pleased with the news, a smirk spreads wide across my face.

Work is done for the day, and it looks like I'm actually getting paid.

Suddenly, I don't want to go straight home. I'm in the mood to celebrate—to the coffee shop I go.

Six

Arielle

"Graham's wife had a boy, and they named him Vincente," Christian reports from the high-top table he's been sitting at all morning. The power has been restored, but since Graham couldn't come in, we offered to help again. We are on day two of running this place, and we've quickly settled into a pattern, where Christian "works" on his laptop, and I help all the actual customers.

It's fine though.

Keeping my hands moving is preventing me from thinking about Tom. Whoops, I just thought of him again. He's sneaky like that. Also, the people in this little town are the sweetest. I've learned a lot about this place. Like, how they have a new AHL hockey team that is extremely bad, but the town loves them anyway. Or how they have a famous restaurant called Red Barn Kabobs that started in an actual barn. I've learned so many random facts about this place from the small-town gossip mill, but the thing I'm most curious to know about is that lumberjack who was in here yesterday.

He's so different from any of the men I see in Boston, and he had this easygoing way about him, despite how huge and scary he should have looked. It was oddly alluring. I've found myself peeking out the window every few minutes, hoping to see his truck at the park.

"You're not hoping Tom is going to show up, are you?" Christian parks a hand on his hip, his big brother tone firing in all decibels. "I know you think you love him, but I guarantee if I ever see his scrawny little body again, I'm going to make sure he knows he's not welcome."

"No." My brows furrow together. "Of course not—" I stop myself because I don't care to argue. Something about being out here in the mountains is a respite from so many things, including any desire I would normally feel to defend myself. I didn't know it when we first set out for this place, but it was exactly what I needed. "I'm watching the snow, wondering if we are going to leave tomorrow."

"We better." Christian slams his laptop shut and slips off the stool with urgency. "I need to be back on Long Island for a food vendor show. It's the largest one of the year, and I'm hoping to snag some more catering clients." Christian flashes his phone screen at me, and a swaddled-up baby stares at me.

"Aw, cute." I smile at the photo, as if the baby can see my big cheesy grin through the phone. "I'm glad mom and baby are safe."

"Graham says he'll be back to work tomorrow for part-time hours." His brows lower as he reads his phone. "What is this? I have a text message I didn't see." He taps on his phone, reading aloud, "'The Coffee Loft truck will be here in five minutes.' Oh, man." His gaze jerks to the backdoor where the loading dock is. "We might have to lock up early." He scoops up his laptop, stuffing it into the backpack he always carries. "The truck is bringing all our Coffee Loft branding. I can't wait to see it because they are transitioning to a new color scheme of blue and cream. After it's set up, I'll need to shut down for a few days. I'll have a huge grand opening in the next couple of weeks." He zips his bag and slips it onto his back. "That will happen on the next trip though. I can't be gone that long. I've put an ad in the newspaper for an assistant manager's position. It's best if I leave it open for at least a week. Then I can come down to interview and hopefully hire and train." His eyebrows wag playfully at me as he drops his voice, pretending to add an evil inflection when he says, "It's all part of my master plan."

An assistant manager position.

I sort of like the sound of that.

It definitely has a better ring than "my dad's cleaning lady."

I'm not sure why I never thought of working for Christian for real before, but I could easily get used to this little town. The thing is, if I say something about it now, Christian will think I'm running away from my problems. My jaw twitches, begging me to offer to take the job, but I don't take the bait. It's too soon. I need to show him I'm serious about the job, and not just about hiding out.

The door whips open, pulling my gaze with it. My heart instantly thrums against my chest to see the same imposing, bearded man who was in here yesterday. "Good morning." I bite my lip, trying to keep from smiling too large as I sneak a glance at his forearms.

"Good morning." He nods to Christian, who is hurrying to the back, and waves on his way out to meet the truck.

The man's eyes are fast to meet mine. My heart skips a beat when he doesn't look away. I swallow and move my feet until I'm behind the coffee bar. "Nice to see you again. What can I get you?"

He's slow to pull his gaze away from me and onto the menu. "I guess that depends if you have coffee today?"

"So sorry." I shake my head and stare off in the direction Christian just left. "We are transitioning to a Coffee Loft franchise. My boss decided rather than fix the equipment, he's waiting to install the new stuff." I pull my lips into a big smile, hoping to smooth everything over. I'm not sure why I care so much about making this man happy, but he's huge. I would hate to see him grumpy. Especially if he hasn't had his coffee yet. "Tomorrow," I rush out. "We'll have our new stuff and trust me." I lean in, as if I'm letting him in on a secret, "We'll have our signature Coffee Loft blends. Once you try those, the wait will all be worth it."

His lips straighten into a neutral expression. Under his thick beard, it's hard to read if he's upset. I hate to warn off customers when we haven't even officially opened. "How about this?" I blurt out, hoping he doesn't leave upset. "I'll make whatever tea you want, and it's on me today, but you have to promise to come back tomorrow to try the coffee."

"You're asking me to come back tomorrow?" His dark eyes hover over mine, tension rising between us, and my heart beats hard against my chest.

"F-For coffee," I stutter.

His broad shoulders move up and down and he stares deeply into my eyes, as if he can feel how hard my heart is beating. The silence drags on past a normal pause into something that feels like a challenge, a languid flirtation with so much deep eye contact, it affects my breathing. "I guess I'll stop back tomorrow." His words are smooth, easy.

His gaze drives my adrenaline to rapid fire through my veins, and it makes me feel attractive in a way that Tom never made me feel. He never looked at me like that. All I want to do is think of something witty to banter back, but that's not something I've ever been good at. "You'll be glad you did because you'll love it," I finish in my best professional tone, despite my heart hammering out beats. I swallow and carry on in my happy-to-serve-you voice. "How about another tea like I made you yesterday?"

"That would be great." His gaze drifts to the floor for a moment before he lifts it back to me. "I, ah, am sorry I didn't get a chance to talk to you yesterday when you came over to the park. Was there something you needed?"

I can feel a warm blush creep on my cheeks as that whole scene was so cringe. I had tried to talk to him, but clearly, I wasn't the only woman vying for his attention. I guess I'm not the only one who thinks he's handsome. Sighing, I answer with the safest answer I can, "No, I was out on a walk for some fresh air, and thought I'd say hi."

"Well, either way, I'm sorry we got interrupted," he says. I struggle not to stare at his hands when he offers me his card. I pass his cup over, and our fingertips brush together. I can't help but think that was intentional—on both our parts. Goosebumps spiral up my arm as we hold each other's gazes. They are joined by a magnetism I've never felt. We reluctantly exchange goodbyes. When he leaves the store, my heart beats so rapidly, it's like I just worked out.

"Relax," I breathe out, letting my shoulders fall as I scold myself.

This is ridiculous to be this flustered.

I'm obviously overly emotional about Tom still and have forgotten how to have normal interactions with men. I shake my head as I reach for a towel and wipe my sweating palms off.

Get a grip, girl.

It's just a man.

A gorgeous and muscular man, whose smile has the power to stop my heart—that's all.

And besides, I've sworn off dating—forever.

My gaze makes a circular arc around the tops of my eyes as I rethink that. All I can think of is that man's smile.

Well . . . maybe not forever.

Just until I get over Tom.

Seven

Stallone

I wake up abruptly with sweat pouring off my chest. The sunrays peek under my window's pale shade, revealing I've slept to a normal time.

I blink.

This is a strange anomaly, but wonderful, as I can already tell I'm more rested than normal. My joints move with an ease they haven't had in a long time, and I spring up.

It's also bad because Ryson will be waiting for me.

I scurry to get dressed while Lucky hangs back in the hall, pacing between the bathroom and the kitchen. He's not quite sure what to think about our change of routine. I'm in such a hurry, I don't have time to think about it either and pull up to Ryson's cabin with a screech of my brakes.

Ryson's smile is pressing as he hops in and patiently waits for Lucky to plop on his lap. He gives me the side-eye. "Did you go out last night?"

"No." Instant irritation kills my grin, and I take a defensive tone. "I actually slept for once."

"Ah, too bad." His expression falls to a woeful one as his hand lazily pets Lucky.

"What do you mean it's too bad I slept?" I'm immediately annoyed, as Ryson does not know what I've been through this year. He's never had a relationship that lasted longer than a slow country western song, and he surely doesn't know what it's like to have your fiancée leave you right before the wedding. A wedding we took a year to plan together, and all our friends and family were already in town, ready to help us celebrate.

"Not that it's bad you slept." His eyes roll, but his voice softens. "Just that I thought maybe you went out for once."

"What does it matter?" I clench the steering wheel and peel out of his driveway. Everyone has a timeline for me. They all think I should move on, but what they don't know is I have my own timeline: one that says, I don't care if I ever move on.

"Have you even gone on one date yet?" He stares forward, as if he knows not to dare challenge that question with direct eye contact.

Tongue-tied, fire ignites in my chest, and I stomp on the brakes, bringing my truck to a screeching halt before I managed to blurt, "What do you want from me?" I glare at him like he's my nagging mother, and not the little brother who I helped raise.

"I want you to be happy." His dark eyes that match mine level with me. "You deserve it."

I swallow, as he has no idea what I deserve, and I steer the wheel straight again and press on the accelerator, grumbling, "Mind your own business."

We are silent until we get to the jobsite, and I don't hesitate to jump out of the truck to run to the timber crane. I can't wait to be alone, and I mutter, "Ryson doesn't have a clue what will make me happy."

EIGHT

Arielle

"My job here is done." Christian zips his black hardcover suitcase up and slides it off the hotel bed. Brushing his hands together, he plants a pleased smile on his face. "Do you have your stuff together? They opened the interstate, and I'd like to get on the road by nine."

I'm having the hardest time crawling out of bed, and I struggle to keep my eyes open. My body decided to take up permanent residence in this spot, despite the many times I've rubbed my eyes and stretched. "Yeah, I just need to grab my stuff out of the bathroom." I roll over, letting one foot hang to the floor, testing an upright position.

Ert.

Nope.

I pull it back onto the bed and sigh. "Do we have to leave so early?"

"You don't have to go back to Boston." Christian's words are measured, as if he's rehearsed this speech. "You can stay with me if you want. It might be helpful to have an extra hand in the store since I'll be returning here in a few days."

"Oh, wait a second . . ." My brows bead together as I visualize the return to Long Island today. I sit up straight as I recall inviting that man to come back today. It was a casual comment I made to prevent him from being upset. I hadn't thought that we wouldn't even be here. That was a hairbrained thing to do. I scratch the back of my head, lazily speaking through a deep yawn. "I did something dumb. I was so eager to get the new Coffee Loft equipment yesterday, I told the customers to come back to try the coffee today."

"Why would you do that?" Christian parks a hand on his hip, never disappointing when it comes to all-things dramatic.

"I wasn't thinking clearly." I rub my eyes and yawn one more time as I stand and stare at the bathroom, all the way over on the other side of the room. It feels like a lot of effort right now.

"We can stop by on the way out of town. I can put a sign on the coffee bar explaining we're closed to prepare for a grand reopening."

My gaze directs to the tiny hotel window, the tops of
the distant snow-covered mountain range peeking out
from behind the downtown buildings. I feel so different
in Mapleton. My chest isn't as tight as it was back home,
and I can take real breaths. I'm in a little bubble that's safe
from real life. When I think about going back to Long
Island—even though it's not Boston—I think about reality hitting. I'm not ready to hurt again. "You know," I
say slowly, already positive Christian will hate my idea. "I
could stay."

His head cocks to the side, and he freezes. "Why would
you do that?"

I lift one shoulder into an anticlimactic shrug. "I can
keep the coffee bar open, and you won't lose customers
from being closed. Maybe I could even screen the job ap-
plicants for you?"

"I would be tempted to take you up on the offer if I
didn't think you were using this as an excuse to hide from
reality." Christian's mouth takes a downward angle as his
eyes pace my face. "I don't think that's healthy."

"Just for a week." My voice cracks, as I hate explaining
to Christian, of all people, how I'm a classic avoidant personality type. I would rather just deal with my heartbreak
my way—by pretending it didn't happen.

He whips his head to the side. I'm sure he's about to
roll it back in a hard "no" shake, but instead, his gaze finds

mine and he's unusually soft in his tone. "I'm going to worry about you if I leave you here."

"I'll be fine," I say, my voice barely above a whisper. "Just let me take this time for myself."

His lips bunch to the side, into a hard thinking position, before he heaves a heavy sigh. "Call me immediately if you hear from Tom."

I nod, my lips bending as I know he's already giving in.

"If Dad finds out, tell him I had nothing to do with this. I'll be back on Sunday to take you home." He removes his keys from his coat pocket and slides one off the ring for me, handing it over. "To the bookstore. Don't lose it."

"I won't." I reach for my boho-style bag on the nightstand, retrieve my key ring, and slide it on. I don't have many keys on the ring, but one that stands out is the key to Tom's place. My lips paste into a frown. I'm not sure why he ever gave it to me because I wasn't allowed to use it without first letting him know I was coming. My frown doesn't abate, instead my brows lower, tipping my expression into a scowl. I had overlooked another clue to his infidelity that was right in front of my face. My cheeks heat from the pure anger that's left at all the lies he told me and for taking advantage of me. My fingers move with precision to slide that key off the ring, and I cup it in my palm and walk it over to the trash.

If I wasn't trying to keep my cool in front of Christian to install confidence that I actually am fine, I might have tried to do something more dramatic with this key. Not sure what, but slamming it over and over with a hammer might have been fun.

Christian doesn't see me toss it away because he's typing on his phone. After a moment, he says, "I let Graham know you'll be staying."

"I'm not a little girl." A chuckle twitches from inside, as I had forgotten how protective Christian can be of me. It's one result of us growing up together without a mother. I playfully shoo him away. "Leave. I'll be fine. Better than fine. I'll have the coffee shop deep cleaned and running at full speed by the time you get back."

And maybe I'll have a new friend by then too—One who has excellent taste in flannel shirts. My heartbeat picks up the pace as I tease the idea.

"I'll stop at the front desk to request they extend the stay in this room." He grips his suitcase handle, pulling it behind him as he stops right before the door. "I don't mean to rush, but I really do need to get to my vendor show."

"And to Portia." I smile teasingly at him, as I'm so happy he has someone to rush home to.

"And to Portia." His smile matches mine, but he doesn't pause for a beat when he adds, "You'll find your happily ever after too." His eyes spring open, and he tacks on, "Just don't let Portia know you're looking, or she'll add you to her website."

"I already told her I wasn't interested in ever going on that website." I flash my hands up in a silent wave, because if I don't end this, Christian will stay all morning "making sure I'm okay." He'll miss his vendor show. "Love you."

Flashing his palm up in a wave, he says, "I'll call you later."

"Bye."

Bowing his head, he opens the door, pulling the suitcase behind him. I wait for the door to click and turn on my heel, heading to the window. I'm not sure what I'm expecting to see. People bustle in and out of the downtown shops, carrying perfect little packages filled with the treasures they found, all wearing smiles on their faces. That part is enjoyable to see, but the best part is that none of these people know me or Tom. That's exactly the kind of place I need to be right now. I cross the room to my suitcase and pull out a pair of faded jeans and a cream sweater and head to the shower.

Today is going to be a good day.

Because I said so.

And maybe, a handsome guy will come in for coffee.

It's ten minutes to six o'clock, and I shut off the brightest overhead lights as the last two customers head out. It's been a slow day with the bookstore remaining closed. I assume most of the town residents are yet to find out about the new partnership with Coffee Loft. That makes sense to me since Christian hasn't done any advertising. I open the cash drawer to count the bills. Like clockwork, as soon as I stop thinking that *maybe* he'll come in, the door swings open, and my heart skips a beat.

"Am I too late?" My lumberjack peeps inside. He's wearing a heavy blue flannel shirt and jeans, looking as casual as can be, but the way he immediately finds my gaze and holds it sparks the butterflies in my gut.

"No, not at all." I push the cash back into the drawer and close it with my hip. "I was hoping you'd stop by."

"I told you I would." He steps forward, letting the door jingle to a close behind him. "You owe me a coffee."

"I do." Heat flushes my cheeks as everything about the way this man looks at me makes my knees jelly. "Have a seat." I gesture forward, adding in a playful tone, "Let me guess how you like your coffee."

He pulls up the closest barstool, plopping down, both eyes locked on me. "Not with tea."

"How about something sweet?"

"I like my coffee so strong my ancestors can taste it." His chuckle slips out at the exact time mine does: his baritone sound perfectly balances my sweet inflections.

"Maybe just a little sweet then." I scan all the new Coffee Loft syrups displayed behind me until I catch the perfect one, or in this case two. I've never been one to initiate any kind of flirting, but since no one knows me here, I seem to have found the confidence to be a little bold. I grab the marshmallow and the raspberry and hold them up. "If I mix these together, and add a little milk, you get something called a raspberry kiss." I hold my gaze steady on him and bite back a smile as he squirms in his seat, shifting from side to side.

He doesn't disappoint, flirting right back. "It's our first coffee together, and you're already offering a kiss." He lets his direct eye contact linger.

It's suddenly apparent the heat in this place is definitely working at full steam today. I push up my sweater sleeves to my elbows, all the while wishing I could crack a window open. "Technically, this is my *third* time serving you." I set the syrups on the counter and grab a large drink cup, the one we call the Lofty size. I don't care what size he orders, but I'm giving him a free upgrade. I tip the empty cup toward him. "This one is on me for all the trouble this week." After sidestepping to the espresso machine, I push the button for the espresso before I ask, "Caffeine good or do you need decaf?"

"The only time I've ever gotten decaf coffee to work for me is the time I threw it at my brother." He holds a straight face, but as hard as I try to bite back a laugh, a snort bleeps out. He acknowledges my snort with a simple, "That's classy."

"It really wasn't." I pump the syrups into the cup, add the milk and espresso, mixing it all together. A gleam in his eye sparkles when I set the coffee in front of him, and it encourages me.

I hate for this conversation to be over.

I spent all day looking out the window for him, and now *it's over*. He's so fun to banter with, and it's been ages since I let myself do this. I point to the coffee-mug shaped clock on the wall, now one minute past six. "I have to lock up, but if you don't have anywhere to go, you're welcome to sit with me while I clean." I hold my breath, unsure where my sudden bravery came from.

"I really should be on my way." His gaze regretfully pulls to the exit, and my heart drops. How did I get this conversation so wrong?

He was totally flirting with me.

Maybe he is dating that lady in the park or someone else? My gaze drops to his hands. Not a ring on any of his fingers, but I dare to ask, "Are you involved with someone?"

His lashes flicker, blinking several times. The time it takes for him to answer my question makes me wish I hadn't asked. My fingers get jittery, and I reach for the bar towel for something to fidget with. I direct my gaze down and wipe the counter before I hear his down-hearted reply, "I was, and not looking for anything."

I raise my gaze up to meet his. "Me too, and me neither." I add a shoulder shrug. "Or maybe just a friend."

His Adam's apple bobs, marking his swallow. I stand back, waiting for him to get up and leave. To my surprise, he lifts his drink and takes a sip. He swallows slowly, like he's savoring the flavors, before he sets down his cup. His lips tug up gently in the corners. "Your kiss is very sweet."

"Too sweet?" I park my hand on my hip, feeling the tension rise back up between us.

"It could be perfect." He nods more to himself as his gaze is locked on his drink. "I might need to try another one tomorrow. Just to make sure."

"I'm here all week," I speak softly, as if I'm afraid to stir the air. We'd somehow built a bridge of camaraderie without even trying. I know I could use a friend. Especially one who is as handsome as he is. "My name's Arielle, by the way, but people call me El."

"I think we are doing this backward." He rises to his feet. "You're supposed to tell me your name before you give me your kiss."

I've never met a man who can make my knees shake from just the way he looks at me, but I place my hands on the counter to steady myself. "You can give me the kiss back if you don't want it," I tease, batting my lashes as I gaze up at him.

"Nah, I never said that." He snickers, his gaze drifting from his drink to me. "My name is Stallone."

"Stallone." My smile is flirty, languid. The heat from our direct contact melts my insides. That is such an unusual name, but it suits him well. "Did your parents love *Rocky* movies?"

"My dad was a fan." He shifts his weight from one leg to another, as if he is unsure if he's coming or going. "I'd better let you lock up."

Disappointment trickles into my heart, and I lower my gaze to the bar towel again, saying, "Thanks for stopping in."

"Night." His tone is laced with confusion, and he turns and lumbers out the door. I stare after him.

How did I get that so wrong?

I thought he was coming to see me, but maybe he really did just want coffee.

Nine

Stallone

A battle rages between my head and my heart. My head scolds me, telling me not to go back there. I definitely don't need to get caught up in some weird flirtation.

My heart is quieter, yet somehow stronger, saying, "She's one you won't want to pass up."

I get no sleep.

I'm up even earlier than usual. I fumble through work, all because I have only one thing on my mind.

Arielle and her sweet kiss.

Okay, that's two things, and it's all I think about. One doesn't offer a drink named kiss to another if it doesn't have some sort of innuendo, right? There are rules about that kind of thing.

After work, I lose control over my legs and drive right to the coffee shop. Butterflies spark alive in my gut as soon as I see El is working—and better yet—it's closing time.

We are alone.

I march up to the bar and drop my palms on the counter. "I'll have one of your sweet kisses."

"You're in luck." She bats those flirty and superfluous lashes at me, not missing a beat. "I've been saving an extra sweet one for you all day."

That certainly makes my mouth water.

It's been ages since I've allowed myself to banter with a woman. The innocent smile she gives me when she moves in front of the espresso machine makes my heart putter in full throttle. It's like I've been sleeping too long. I'm finally feeling what it's like to be awake.

"How was your day?" she yells over the milk frother, giving me her sweetest smile. My knees weaken, and I match her smile.

"It was good." I nod, and then nod again. It's silly to be here flirting like a teenager, but I can't resist. "Except I was thinking about your kisses all day."

"Good. I like them to be memorable." Her demure brows rise, and she steps to the side, adding the rest of the ingredients to the cup. She pops the lid on and sets the cup in front of me. "Try this one. It's the leprechaun kiss."

"Leprechaun?" I lift the cup and snicker right over the top of it. The drink heat seeps through the thin cardboard, warming my hands, and I hold it steady and enjoy the thawing.

"They're minty." She tips her chin up, exposing her long neck momentarily before her hand curls around it in a resting position. "Let me know what you think, but I'm guessing you'll like this one even better."

Her lips pinch in anticipation as I lift the cup to my lips and sip. It's toasty, and rich with chocolate coffee notes, and it pulls me even more awake. I lower my cup and say with a straight face, "Definitely lucky."

The sweetest chuckle rolls out of her lips. Her gaze levels with mine, and my heart hammers against my chest wall as I feel this human connection I haven't felt in forever. I pull the stool out and plop down and make a dramatic eye sweep to the clock behind us. "Are you closing?"

She slowly nods, and her voice drops to a low hum. "I need to."

I could be wrong, but I've seen this look before. It's the way she looked yesterday when she asked me to stay, and it makes me weak in the knees. "I could stay if you want company while you clean."

Her perfect white teeth slide over her bottom lip, and she bites down, holding that pose for a moment. "I actually have everything cleaned already."

"Oh." I sit up straight and rotate on the stool so my legs angle toward the door. "Ah, that's fine. I got stuff to—"

She reaches over the counter and places her hand on mine. Fireworks explode right in my palm—no exaggeration. I struggle to feel my skin as she says, "I got all my cleaning done early, because I was hoping you'd want to hang out."

The heat from her hand zips all the way up my arm and doesn't stop until it makes a nice ring around my heart. "Okay," is all I can manage.

"I thought we could have coffee together." She grabs a coffee that was sitting on the back counter, waiting for her. "I made one for myself." She gestures toward the table up front next to the window. "Is that okay?"

"Sure." I rise to my feet, and we drift together as we cross the room. Now I'm wishing I'd put on my good aftershave, the one I haven't worn in a year. Too late for that. I take a deep breath as a light row of perspiration layers on my lower back.

She gingerly slides into her seat, and I plop down across from her, and when our gazes slide together, everything else fades away. My nerves instantly melt because it's the most natural feeling in the world to sit across from her. She leans over her coffee cup and blows into the drink hole before asking, "How was work?"

I blink, hardly even remembering work. It's impossible to think about anything but her gorgeous pale-blue eyes when I'm sitting this close to her. "It was work. How about you?"

"It was wonderful." She runs her hand over her hair, tucking one of her wild strands back behind her ear with a dainty twist of her wrist. It's mesmerizing to watch the way she moves with such feminine grace. "I love being here, and I'll be sad when I have to leave."

Wait. What? She's leaving?

My hand finds my chin, and I rub my beard while I rewind my memories. "I remember you said you were new to town but guess I didn't realize you weren't staying."

She slouches back in her seat, appearing to get more comfortable. "I'm from Boston but was looking to stay in Long Island with my brother for a while when he decided to open this store. My brother is my boss, and well, he's not actually my boss, because I don't officially work for Coffee Loft. It's just easier to call him that." Her words trail off into an airy laugh.

"Interesting." I can feel my brows bunch together, all while a sting digs into my chest, and I repeat, "I didn't realize you're leaving."

She nods, her head bouncing several times into the silence. "Yeah, Sunday will be my last day."

I clear my throat, wishing it was that easy to clear the sting in my chest. "Then I guess we should make use of the time we have together getting to know each other."

"Right." Her tone is flirty and even, not disappointing at all.

I bite my lip, oddly feeling a tinge of relief. I was never looking for anything more than a little flirting. It's actually quite perfect. We can hang out, but nobody gets attached. "So..." I return my cup to the table and lean forward. "Who else is enjoying your kisses?"

"Excuse me?" Her head springs back before she blinks and sputters out a laugh. "You mean the coffee, right?"

I shrug playfully, leaning forward. "Maybe."

"Well, for the coffee-flavored kisses, I've actually saved that recipe for you, and for the uh, other kind of kisses"—her gaze dips to the floor before she rushes out—"I just had a breakup a few days ago, so nobody at the moment, which is how I like it."

I stay quiet but maintain a full smile teasing my lips. She's been flirting with me, so I give it right back.

"What about you?" she quips back, her posture extra tall, and her gaze is pointed. "I know you're single, but it sounds like you had a recent breakup too."

"Ah." My breath is heavy as it crawls up my throat and forms the words. "Not real recent." Her gaze dances around my face, softening as the silence drags on, but she doesn't ask for more clarity. I suppose I could drop it, or change the subject, but as her expression continues to warm, she starts to feel like a friend—someone I could confide in. Maybe it's a mistake, but she'll be gone soon. I haven't spoken about this to anyone other than Ryson.

For a reason I will never understand, I test the words I've never even dared to speak. "I was engaged."

Her lips form an O, but no sound leaks out.

"She left me suddenly a few days before our wedding." My words are steady and surprisingly easy to express. My chest literally releases the tension that's been there for months. "We never even fought. I had no idea, but I guess she had been talking to an ex-boyfriend for a while, and she wanted to be with him."

"I'm so sorry to hear that." El's eyes swell rounder and her hand slides across the table, not stopping until it's on top of mine. "I actually know exactly how you feel. My last boyfriend was cheating on me too."

"You definitely didn't deserve that." My instinct is to go off about how it's okay she left, because she showed me how evil women are, and I dodged a bullet, but El's hand is still on mine. A spiral of heat flows up my arms, melting those thoughts into nothing but air that makes it easy for me to breathe.

I don't know how, but I allow my lips to slide over my teeth into a small smile. "You're going to be okay." A thick tension in the air, and neither one of us bends a lip upward, but our gaze is held together as we both seem to study each other from across the table.

Thud. Thud. Thud.

A rapping on the window pulls our gaze to it, and El immediately gasps. "Look, a dog!"

Not just any dog.

My dog.

Apparently, he got bored sitting in the box of my truck. The evidence is the fact he's covered from head to tail in clinging snow. His paws completely caked in ice clumps frozen to his fur, and paw prints marking his path from my truck to a huge snow pile at the corner—which he apparently rolled in—back to the window. Now he stares with gleeful mischief in his eyes, as if he's proud of how messy he is. His huge eyes peer directly through the window, like he can't take his eyes off El.

I know the feeling.

She's that showstopping.

Everything about the way her hair frames her perfect face makes it impossible not *to stare*. She's just so unbelievably stunning. My heart rams against my chest being near her. "Yeah." My smile grows even wider. "That's my dog. His name's Lucky. I think he's being impatient and was trying to find me. I had him in my truck. I guess he just hopped out." Shrugging, I add, "He's mesmerized by you."

Her airy laugh leaks out of her lips. "I don't know why."

My chest pinches tighter, warning me not to say the words that are about to roll out of my mouth. Not because they are mean, but quite the opposite. I swallow and say, "I know why."

There's still a hint of laughter in her voice when her gaze pulls playfully to mine. "Why's that?"

"He's never seen a woman as beautiful as you." Her mascara-clad lashes flutter but our eye lock holds steady, and I can count the beats of my heart slamming against my chest. "I clearly speak dog."

She throws her head back as her dense laugh fills the air. It's a beautiful sound that sparks a chuckle to form from deep in my chest, and I join her in her laughter. It's been a long time since I laughed like this. It's so effortless to sit here with her. Her gaze slides back to the window, where Lucky still lingers. "If you speak dog, can you tell him it's rude to stare? It's making me a little nervous."

"I can't tell him that." I slide to the edge of my seat, steeling my jaw forward. "Because I know how he feels. He's clearly stunned by your beauty. It's your fault."

A rose tint fires on her cheeks, and she shakes her head, matching my gaze. "You're too much."

"I'm too much?" My voice ticks up, adding playful inflections as I jerk my thumb back to Lucky, whose nose is still pressed against the glass. "I'm not the one drooling all over the window trying to get to you." Her giggles fill my confidence, and I playfully tap the glass and say, "Buzz off, Lucky, I saw her first."

Her laughter upticks even more, her shoulders shaking in synchronization. I sit back in my chair and marvel that I could seriously sit here and listen to her for days. When the last of her cackles die into a playful smile, it feeds my ego even more. "Now what did he say?" She raises her brows at me, challenging me.

"He's not happy. He wants to fight me for you." Before I second-guess myself, I take a huge risk and say, "I told him there is no use in fighting, because you've already decided that you're going out with me next."

"Oh, I have, have I?" Her head takes an angled position, but her smile doesn't deflate. "Where are we going?"

"It's a surprise. Tomorrow." I lower my voice, ridding it of all teasing. "After work. I'll pick you up here."

Her lips part, and her tongue slides out and runs along her bottom lip before she says in a soft voice, "You said you weren't looking to get involved with anyone."

"I'm not," I rasp, knowing this decision is about to change everything, but with the way she's looking at me—all the light firing in her eyes—I don't care. "This is us going out to have fun together without the pressure of dating."

I glance back at the window, but Lucky has walked away and is loitering by my truck, sniffing the tires.

"So, just going out to have fun?" Her heated gaze pulls mine back to her.

I swallow and reply, "Yes."

"Okay." Her bottom lip pushes out, making it incredibly hard not to notice how plush and kissable it is. "I get off work at six. You can meet me here."

"I'll be here." I tip up my cup and finish the last of my coffee, and as I'm trying not to wear out my welcome, I slide off my chair.

"Are you leaving?" Her gaze follows me as I walk to the trash to throw away my empty cup.

"It's time. I don't want my dog to get run over, and he's clearly asking for some trouble since he wants to hang out in the road." I walk to the door and pause to hit her with a direct gaze one more time, taking a moment to linger. Then I put my hand on the door handle and push it ajar. "See you tomorrow, El."

"Bye," she calls after me, and I leave the shop, all the while my heart is slamming against my chest.

What did I just do?

I didn't want to go out with anyone.

She just has this power over me. As soon as I sat next to her, I couldn't help it. I shake my head as I stride to my truck, my eyes peeled for Lucky, who's taken it upon himself to dig in the snow right by my front tire. "Get in, boy." I open the driver's door and wait for him to scurry into the passenger seat. Then I get in and say to him, "I have a date to get ready for."

Ten

Arielle

The coffee shop is agonizingly slow. I prop both elbows on the counter, rest my chin in my palms and sleepily stare out the window, wishing customers would come in. I honestly think everyone assumes since Graham isn't here, the place is closed. With nothing else to do, I think about my non-date tonight and now my gut wads into a ball of nerves.

It's been so long since I hung out with a new guy, especially one this handsome.

What if I say something dumb?

Really, it's not even a "what-if" for me, but more like how many times something embarrassing will slip out. I don't want to get all worked up about it though, so it ruins my chances of having fun. I let out a sharp sigh, refusing to let my nerves get the best of me, and I open my phone, ready to scroll.

The karaoke app finds my attention, which makes me smirk. I haven't needed the distraction since I met Stallone. It's crazy how things can change in just a few days. Now it just looks like something I could do to pass some time. With my free hand I drum my nails on the counter. I'm not huge into karaoke but if they are playing the right song, it might be fun.

I might as well check it out.

I tap on the screen to see what my first challenge is, and my song appears: "Fishing in the Dark."

I let out a haughty laugh. I know that song and could sing it in my sleep. Challenge accepted. Rolling my shoulders back, I do a warm up stretch as I wait for the timer to count down. The screen changes, and I'm thrown into a challenge room, and I start singing.

I'm not going to say I could be rockstar material, but I've definitely found my rhythm, and I take down the first challenger—no problem. I really hope he doesn't cry because he honestly never had a chance.

I advance to another level, and another after that. I just keep going, and my competitive side comes out without apologies. I'm taking out everyone.

All afternoon I keep advancing and leveling up. I sing so many songs, and I dominate. I don't know why I have never tried karaoke before, but this is really a hobby I could enjoy more often. One thing I figure out is I especially excel at anything Disco.

It's my genre.

I'm two verses into ABBA's "Dancing Queen" when Christian calls me. I literally growl at his name on my phone as it forces me to forfeit my round. I hate doing that, but I'm so far ahead of everyone else. Even if I forfeit this round, I can win the overall tournament. "I'm fine," I assert as soon as I answer the phone.

"Whoa, what's wrong with you?" His big-brother tone passes through my phone. "I wanted to make sure you had enough cash in the till, since you haven't been doing any bank runs."

"I'm fine." I quickly pop the drawer open to confirm there's plenty of change and cash, especially since no one has come in today. After a second eye sweep, I press the drawer closed. "I know how to go to the bank if I run out." I sneak a peek at the time. The app sends me an invite when it's time for my next challenge, and it could be anywhere from one minute to a half hour, depending on how everyone else sings.

I can't miss my invitation.

"I don't know." He sounds panicked. "I really shouldn't have left you there. I think it's best if we close the store until we get ready to do the grand opening—"

"It's fine," I mutter again as I wonder how many times I can repeat the same exact sentence in one conversation.

"I'm getting to know your customers." *Well, only one of your customers, and he's quite nice.* My lips curl into an amused smile at the mere thought of Stallone.

"I know how you are when you are going through a breakup. You get unpredictable mood swings. You keep saying you're fine, but"—he stalls for a beat— "but are you, really?"

"Yes." I soften my tone, hoping he finally believes me. "And if it makes you feel better, I promise if I'm not fine, I will let you know."

"Do you really promise?"

"I do." I pace back and forth behind the counter, my fingers itching to end the call. "Trust me, it's so good for me to be here alone, because nothing here reminds me of Tom. I haven't even once thought of him. I'm pretty much over him."

A heavy sigh passes through the phone and relief fills his voice. "That's good to hear."

"It is."

"Okay, you've convinced me for now, but don't hesitate to call if you need anything."

"Of course." The edges of my lips bend into a larger smile. "Love you, bye."

"Bye, El."

I end the call and swipe my screen to see I'm still in the hold queue. "Phew," I breathe out. "I didn't miss my round." Lifting my gaze to scan the coffee shop, I'm further relieved to see there are no customers inside and no one even remotely close to the door. This place is beyond dead. I don't know what I'd do all day without this app.

Since nobody comes to the coffee shop, I keep accepting karaoke challenges. After winning my twenty-fifth challenge in a row, it's time to lock up. It's perfect timing too, because I need to refresh my makeup before Stallone arrives. Some of these choruses make me work up such a sweat; my eye makeup has been long gone.

I set my phone down and reach under the counter for my purse and pull out my sparkly pink makeup pouch. I carry little makeup with me. Just the essentials, so it's easy to find my finishing powder right on top and my favorite lipstick. I blot all the oily spots on my face with fresh powder and apply my lipstick when a message pops on my phone.

CONGRATULATIONS ON BEATING 25 CHALLENGES! YOU ARE CURRENTLY IN SECOND PLACE. IF YOU WIN THE LIGHTNING ROUND, YOU WILL BE THE ULTIMATE CHAMPION AND WIN $500.

DO YOU ACCEPT THIS LIGHTNING ROUND CHALLENGE? YES OR NO.

My eyes round with excitement. *Five hundred dollars!* Up until now, I've only been accumulating those fake diamonds. I somehow passed the threshold into the rounds where I can win actual money. I'm not one to get excited about the possibility of prize money, but since I made no tips today, and I haven't been to my actual job in days, that money could certainly be useful. My rent isn't going to pay for itself. I've always been a competitive person. I love winning, but the thought of winning money now when I need it the most is appealing. My gaze hangs on the word *champion*—so enticing.

I can see my name next to that word, and the mere thought of it makes saliva pool in the center of my mouth.

I could be a karaoke champion.

I like the sound of that.

And I'd have an extra five hundred dollars, which means I have even more time before I need to return to work.

My gaze scans the coffee shop.

There's no one here.

I can't take too long because I have a date.

How long is the lightning round?

Lightning is fast.

That's why they call it lightning.

And then I'd be the *champion.*

Without another look around the room, I accept the lightning round challenge. I hold my breath as I wait for my first song to pop up, but instead, the front door swings open.

And I drop my phone to the counter like a hot potato.

Stallone passes through the door and it's like he walks in slow motion. His hair's slicked back like a movie star, and he's wearing dark trousers and a black button-up shirt. The sleeves are rolled up, showing off the corded muscles of his forearms, and he's carrying a bouquet of pink roses. Seeing this gorgeous hunk of a man dressed up and walking toward me with flowers makes my cheeks heat as my lips slide into a full smile. It's been years since I've gotten flowers. Tom always said they were a waste of money.

"I hope you like roses," he greets me with his arms outstretched, and I lean in with one arm to give him a hug. The evergreen scent of his cologne hits me, and it infuses my smile with an even bigger curve. *He smells amazing.* Like the manliest man who could pluck an entire tree from the ground—roots and all—if I asked him to.

"I love them." I lean out of our side hug, accepting his flowers at the same time. "That's so thoughtful of you. Thank you."

"You're welcome." He passes his hand through his dark, rich hair. "I didn't know what kind of flowers you liked, but I wasn't going to let that be an excuse. I wanted to bring you something to make you feel special."

My gaze lingers on his eyes. They are dark and rich like his hair, but even better than that, they are *honest.* Of all the characteristics a person could have, that's the one thing I need the most right now. I press my nose to the center of the bouquet while I walk behind the coffee bar. "Let me put these in water before we leave."

I scan the coffee bar.

I clearly don't have a vase.

The cups are cardboard, and more than likely won't be sturdy enough.

Coffeepot it is!

Smirking, I yank out the empty coffeepot from the base, place it in the deep sink, and turn on the faucet.

"It works." His agreeable smile doesn't leave his face, and my cheeks warm from the magnetism I feel when he's around. "I hope it's okay, but I assumed you'd be hungry, so I reserved a table at The Grove restaurant. It's the nicest place in town."

"That sounds amazing." Shutting off the faucet with one hand, I grab the pot with my other hand and shimmy it over to the back counter, where I remove the plastic off the flowers and arrange them into the pot. They are gorgeous, huge roses that barely fit, but I squeeze them in and take another giant whiff. "They really are lovely." I stop myself from gushing, because it's not like he's my boyfriend or anything.

It just feels nice to be spoiled a little, and I stride toward the coat hook on the back wall, grab my heavy blue coat, and tug on the beanie I wear every day. Then I cross the room again, grab my purse off the counter, and shoulder it. I spot my phone setting on the counter where I had tossed it, and I slide that into my pocket. "I have everything I need."

He's so handsome, dressed all in black, and my gut quibbles as I walk forward and synchronize my steps with his as we stride to the door. "The restaurant is just down the block, so we can walk if you're comfortable," he says.

"That works for me." I tug at my coat and pull the top two buttons through the holes to close it. "I'm getting used to this little town. It seems like everything is mostly within walking distance."

"Downtown has everything you need." He holds the door open, and we pass through it, and then pause on the other side so I can lock it. I stuff my keys back into my purse and look up at him. His hand is outstretched to me. It's a sweet gesture that feels natural, and I take his hand in mine. I bite my bottom lip to keep my jaw from dropping when I struggle to intertwine our fingers together. His hands are so big, it's like I'm holding a bear's paw, but I love it. It's so strong and steady, I'm overcome with the feeling of security. Nothing could ever harm me if I'm near these hands.

We cross the street, walk past a small school and bakery, and arrive at the restaurant. He opens the door for me again, and we meet the host, dressed in a formal white shirt and black pants. The host bops his head as if in a nod of recognition at Stallone as he grabs two menus and immediately says, "Right this way."

As we stroll through the dining room, people slide their gazes to look at us. Several people actually stop chewing as we pass. My cheeks heat, and I remove the beanie from my head, thinking that's the problem.

The stares continue.

The host leads us all the way to the corner booth in the back of the dining room. Gesturing forward, he says to me, "Ladies first."

I slide into my seat, take the menu he hands me, and I listen as he recites the specials: lobster for seventy-nine dollars and filet mignon, also for seventy-nine dollars. After he leaves, I lean over the menu and snicker. "Boy, that doesn't sound like a special for seventy-nine dollars." My gaze falls to the menu, and there isn't a thing on here for less than twenty-five bucks.

This place is expensive.

My gaze slopes back to Stallone reading the menu, unbothered by the prices. I don't have it in me to order anything that costs a whole day's worth of wages. Scanning the menu again, I land on the appetizers and find clam chowder soup for fifteen bucks.

Clam chowder it is.

And just in time. The waiter arrives to take our order. Stallone orders a steak and baked potato, and he watches me closely as I order my soup. I hand my menu back to the waiter and look around the place again.

It's dark in this little corner, with only soft candlelight on our table. I still can't shake the feeling that people are staring at us. I look around, seeing people all dressed in their finest, and decide maybe it's the fact I'm under-dressed. I can't do anything about it now. I clear my throat and lock my gaze back with his. "How was work today?"

"It was good. The roads finally cleared up enough. They've been a mixture of mud or ice, and that kept us at a standstill for weeks." He takes his water glass and sips out of it before asking, "How was your day?"

"Really slow." I nod as if I'm agreeing with myself. "I don't know if people think the place is closed since Graham closed the bookstore, or if it's always this slow, but I think I only served five people all day."

"Only five people?" His eyes round with interest. "What did you do all day?"

All the song lyrics I belted out scroll through my mind like they are playing on the phone screen, and I almost giggle. "Ah, just looked at my phone all day." I tightly pinch my lips together, holding back a laugh. "Good thing for technology, right?"

"Right." He's so dialed into me, not taking his eyes off me. It feels like we've known each other for much longer than a few days. It doesn't feel like a first date. He clears his throat, and starts slowly, "I know this is forward of me, but I'm curious about something. Can I ask you a question?"

"Sure." My interest is piqued, and I wait.

"I hope you don't take this the wrong way, but from the moment I saw you, I honestly thought you are the most stunning woman I've ever seen. But for the life of me, I can't really tell how old you are. Can I ask your age?"

"Oh." My brows pin together. I thought he had something serious to ask me. My age is nothing. "I just turned twenty-one."

He's just about to take another sip of water, but spits it back into his glass. "Twenty-one?"

"Yeah." My gaze shifts side to side, and my nerves tick up as I clearly missed the punch line. "What's wrong with that? How old did you think I was?"

"I didn't know." He wags his head back and forth and sets his glass out of reach. "I assumed you were older than that, since you worked day shifts at a coffee shop. Maybe twenty-seven or thirty."

"Nope. Not thirty." A chuckle sputters out. That is the funniest thing. "Well, how old are you?"

"Aw, not thirty." He holds my gaze for a moment, and then it dawns on me what he's concerned about.

"You're older than thirty?"

He nods but adds no words.

"How much older than thirty?" My gaze washes over his facial features. It's so hard to tell because of his thick beard. He doesn't have any wrinkles. All his hair is dark, void of any gray. He's seriously so dreamy, he could be a movie star. There's no way he'd be older than thirty-one or thirty-two.

"I'm thirty-five." His tone is even as he stares deeply into my eyes.

"Wow." My head springs back as his words echo. "You don't look that old at all."

He runs his hands over his beard, proudly smoothing his whiskers. "Yeah, I think the beard makes it hard to tell."

"I agree." I marvel at how, again, I had no idea he was *fourteen* years older than me.

One of his brows takes a northerly hike. "Does it bother you I'm that old?"

"No—" I'm interrupted by my phone vibrating in my pocket. Nobody calls me, except for Christian, and I already talked to him today. "Excuse me." I retrieve my phone out and glance at the screen: **Lightning Round Loading...You are a finalist. Your round begins in one minute.**

Oh no!

I had forgotten about my karaoke battle! I was in the holding room the whole time.

"Is everything okay?" Stallone asks.

"Yeah." I hover my thumb over the screen, ready to put it into sleep mode, but then another message flashes on the app.

Your randomly selected genre is: Disco.

My eyebrows shoot to the ceiling.

That's my genre!

Another message: You're randomly selected song is: "YMCA." Your round begins in 30 seconds.

I know that song!

Like not only do I know that song, my friends and I dressed up as The Village People for a talent show one year, and we performed that song. I know everything there is to know about that song.

I could win five hundred dollars and be the ultimate karaoke champion.

"Are you sure everything is okay?" Stallone's voice is so kind, and the look of concern he has for me melts my heart. "You look a little flushed."

"Yeah," I breathe out a heavy breath. "Now that you say it, if you don't mind, I'm feeling a little warm." I look behind me and see a back exit. It doesn't look like anyone's back there. It's more of a loading dock or something. I hate to be rude to step out for a minute, but really, I could seriously use that money. If I won that money, that means I can actually stay in Mapleton even longer, which could help me get to know Stallone even more. I jerk my thumb toward the exit. "If you don't mind, I'm going to step out for some air."

"Are you sure?" His gaze shifts to the back door, and I'm already sliding out of my booth. "I can come with you."

"Nah, I just need five minutes, and I'll be fine." Well, actually four minutes and one second to be exact, but he doesn't need to know I need to belt out a disco song. I beeline to the back and slide through the door right when my round starts. I toss a look over my shoulder as the door latches shut, and I belt out the healthiest "Youngman" anyone has ever heard.

This is my jam!

Not only do I know all the words, but I got the moves.

I hold the phone to my mouth, the lyrics flowing out in perfect timing. With my free arm, I flay out all the motions. I feel it in my soul that I'm going to win this round. It's confirmed when the meter fills all the way with green and confetti falls.

I won the lightning round!

I am the champion.

I ninja kick the air, as this victory is all mine.

Wait.

What?

A message pops up.

You've won round one of three. Your next round starts in fifteen minutes.

What? How come I have to sing again? This must be a scam.

I just won, but clearly it was an elimination round, which means I'm still in the running for the money. Money I could seriously use.

My gaze cuts back to the door. I better get inside because I would hate for Stallone to get the wrong idea and think I'm rude. Plus, I only have fifteen minutes before I have to sing again. I'm so close to winning this thing, there is no way I'm quitting now.

I can almost taste this victory.

Eleven

Stallone

The waiter brings our food, but El hasn't returned to her seat. Clearing my throat, I check behind me at the back door again. She had looked like she was about to be ill. I hated to let her run off alone, but she also looked embarrassed.

Should I check on her?

She was fine when I picked her up. I hope it's not something I said.

Oh wait.

She got sick right after I told her my age.

That has to be it.

She doesn't want to be here with an old man.

I grossed her out.

My gaze slides to the table, and a knot bulges in my throat. I had no idea she was *that* young. It's so hard to tell these days how old women are. Maybe I should apologize and take her home?

She flies around the corner, bringing a gush of cold air in with her, plopping back down into the booth with an enormous smile on her face. "Good, the food's here."

Her porcelain cheeks are tinted with rose, which is normal for just coming inside from the winter air. She looks fine now. Relief floods back over me, and I take my napkin and set it on my lap. "Yeah, you're just in time. Are you feeling better?"

"Much better." She picks up her soup spoon and scoops giant spoonfuls into her mouth in a very rushed manner.

"Isn't it hot too eat that fast?" I lower one eye and narrow my focus. Her eating pattern is a tad strange. I would have thought she'd eat in a more ladylike fashion, but I guess I'm no one to judge.

"I'm so hungry." She pauses and smiles at me before she hovers her face directly over her bowl and shovels in full spoons of soup.

Taking my fork and knife in my hand, I remember my manners as I carefully cut my steak. "Do you want a straw? It might be even faster." I risk a joke because I've never seen anyone eat like that.

She giggles, but still doesn't slow. Now, she's at the bottom of her bowl, and she drags her spoon along the bottom, scraping every last drop. "It was delicious." She sits back in her seat; a victorious expression washes over her face while she dabs the corners of her mouth with her napkin. "Best soup ever. Thanks for bringing me here."

I barely have my meat cut, and her gaze cuts to the front exit like she's waiting to leave. I motion to my full plate. "Are you in a hurry, or do you mind if I eat?"

"Oh." Her brows spring up. "Go right ahead and finish, but if you don't mind, I'm going to use the restroom."

Before I protest, she takes off through the dining room toward the front foyer where the restrooms are, and I stare after her.

Maybe she really is sick but is too embarrassed to say?

Or is she too humiliated to sit next to me because I'm so old?

My gaze drops to my steak again. It looked so juicy and mouthwatering when the waiter brought it over. It's served on an iron skillet and was literally sizzling, wafting off Cajun spices. It took every ounce of strength I had to wait until El was back before I cut into it. Now my stomach is in a knot, my appetite is gone.

What did I do wrong?

It has to be my age.

And honestly, who am I kidding to even drag this out? If I were her, there is no way I'd want to date me. I just need to get real about it.

The waiter comes up and leans over a tad. "Is everything all right with your steak, sir? I noticed you cut it but haven't taken a bite."

"It's fine." I stare at the chunks all neatly sliced, and I know what I need to do. I take my credit card out of my wallet and hand it to him. "I'm ready to settle up, and may I have a to-go box? My *date*—I mean, my dinner companion has gotten ill."

"Certainly." He disappears for a minute before returning with my card and a box. I transfer my meal and secure it in the box, and she's still not back.

I get she may want privacy, but what kind of man am I if I leave her here by herself if she is seriously ill? Maybe I should ask a waitress to check on her? I get up from the table, box in hand, and make my way back through the dining room. I can feel everyone's eyes on me. Living in a small town is hard, because people know your business. I'm sure they are all wondering who the female is.

Right as I get to the front foyer, El stumbles out of the ladies' room, a full layer of sweat on her forehead.

Poor thing.

She must be running a fever.

She really is ill.

Her eyes swell huge when she sees me, and she stutters, "W-What are you doing here?"

"I was going to send a waitress in to check on you." I gesture forward. "I can tell you're not feeling well. I'm sorry you're ill, but I'm happy to take you home so you can rest."

The back of her hand finds her shimmering forehead, and she attempts to wipe the sweat off her brow. "Ah, I didn't mean to mess up our date," she rushes out, her complexion flushing even more.

"You're not messing it up at all." I walk forward until I'm next to her and place a hand on her lower back to guide her toward the exit. "You can't help that you got ill. I'll take you back to the lodge."

"I'm really feeling much better," she rushes out. "Besides, I have at least an hour before—" her voice drops off.

"Before . . . you have a curfew?" I tease.

"No, just ignore that." She lets out a high-pitched laugh that does nothing to conceal her nerves. Then it makes sense.

Maybe she's not sick, but she's nervous?

She didn't get this way until we got to this restaurant. I *had* to bring her to the nicest place in town as I was trying to impress her. She has to notice everyone staring at us. All this just made her nervous.

"Really, I'm fine." She places a hand on my forearm and a sonic boom explodes. "I'm sorry I ruined our dinner, but I'm not ready to go home yet. I'd love a chance to talk some more."

"If you're sure." I linger on the word sure, giving her a chance to back out again, but she dials her gaze into mine.

I feel an intense pull that says there's no way you are taking her home now, so I suggest something more casual than this, and somewhere we can be alone and away from all the stares. "How about we go on a drive through Evergreen Park?"

"That sounds lovely." She steps toward the exit, her voice pepping up.

I follow right on her heels. Now, let's try not to mess up the next half of the date.

TWELVE

Arielle

My back is a bay of sweat, and it's refreshing to step out in fresh air. I just completed the most epic bathroom performance of "Love Shack" that ever went down. There was even a granny in the last stall. Bless her heart, she didn't ask questions when she came out. She gave me a peace sign and washed her hands while I sang. Of course, I advanced to the next round. Now I have about an hour before the final, final showdown.

As ecstatic as I am that I won my battle round, it broke my heart to see Stallone standing outside the bathroom, looking so downhearted. I feel terrible for ditching him, but I honestly hadn't thought going to the bathroom would look so suspicious. He clearly is taking it personally, and I need to make it up to him. I link my hand into his arm and gaze up at him. "Tell me about your hobbies. What do you like to do for fun?"

"I'm basically your classic outdoorsman. I love to hunt, fish, hike, kayak, camp, anything of that sort. That's why I always found Mapleton to be the perfect place for me to live. I have a cabin up in the mountains, and I can literally do it all in my backyard."

"That sounds amazing. I love hiking and fishing too, but I've never been kayaking before." I bat my lashes. "You might have to teach me."

"Well, kayaking is something I definitely prefer to do when it's a little nicer outside, and I'm guessing you'll be gone by spring . . ." His voice trails off, but his smile lingers on me.

I sigh, adding another inhale afterwards, bringing in enough cool air to relax me even more. "I don't know where I'll be this spring," I answer truthfully. We cross the street where he leads me to his truck parked right outside the coffee shop. It's so easy to get around here, and there's virtually no traffic since everything is within walking distance. It's the opposite of Boston. The air is so fresh and clean here, it's impossible not to take deep breaths. "I can't get over how cute this town is."

"Like I said before, it's the perfect town for me." He opens my door, and I hop in while he walks to the other side and gets in. Once inside, he starts the truck and backs up before picking up our conversation. "So, the same question to you." He nudges my elbow with his. The gentle sign of affection just gets me. I've always been a sucker for the little touches. "What are your hobbies?"

"I like to go out." I stare out the window, watching the cobblestone roads turn to gravel as he winds his way around the outskirts of town and heads to the mountains. I don't tell him that in the last year I've only been out with Tom, and I've done a terrible job of keeping friendships.

"Is that all?"

"Ah, family is a big deal to me. My brother, Christian, and I are close, and . . . I love music."

"What kind of music do you listen to?"

My gaze is still glued to the scenic drive. Since arriving in Mapleton, I've only seen the coffee shop and the lodge. It's breathtaking to see the mountains get closer and closer over the horizon. "Anything really, but I'm a sucker for the oldies, like from the sixties or seventies."

"For a second there, I thought you'd say oldies from the nineties, and I was going to stop you because that's my era. I grew up with that stuff."

I chuckle, sneaking a look at him. "Yeah, I think the nineties is old too, considering I was born in 2003, but I never really got into that decade. There's so much aggression."

"Not all of it." His lips pull to the side as if in a thinking stance. "The nineties also had great ballads. I mean, Celine

Dion and Whitney Houston, Boyz II Men, all of that was the nineties."

"Yeah, I see what you're saying." I stuff my hands in my coat pockets as a cold shudder moves through me.

"Are you cold?" He immediately turns the knobs on the heater, cranking it up.

"Thank you." I look up at him, feeling our magnetism growing even stronger. "This is nice."

"Are you still feeling okay?"

"I feel great."

He slows to take a sharp bend in the road, and a vibration tickles my fingertips. My memory is instantly jogged. I was enjoying my date so much I forgot about the final battle round! I whip my phone out of my pocket, and my chest is filled with dread.

I need to sing now!

Five hundred dollars that I could use is on the line. It won't make me rich, but it will help with all the lost wages.

Christian always teases me about how competitive I am. I never really realized it until now. He's so right. I have this burning in my core that says I can't quit now. If I forfeit then my entire day's work will be lost, and I'm so close to being the ultimate champion. My hand finds the door handle, and I shoot a strained expression to Stallone. "Ah, maybe I need some air. Do you mind pulling over for a second?"

"Here?" One of his brows rises above the other as he steers the truck around the bend. "I can't pull over here, because it's too dangerous. Can you roll down the window until I can get to a better spot?"

My phone vibrates again, indicating my genre was named, and I drop my gaze to my lap.

Genre: Nineties

"Stupid nineties," I mutter, now afraid the app was listening to my earlier conversation. It had to be spying. *There's no way that wasn't a coincidence.*

"What did you say?" Now around the bend, Stallone slows the truck and pulls over to the soft dirt shoulder.

"Nothing," I assert louder, my fingers itching to open the door. If my calculations are correct, I only have about a minute before my song starts. A row of thick evergreen trees lines the ditch, and they'll be perfect to tuck behind. I need to run *now.* "You can stop right here. That's fine."

"Can I help you at all or—"

"Nope." I shove the door open, and drop to the ground, calling back, "I just need three minutes." I dart forward, but the ground is soft and muddy, and I cannot get my footing. I slip and slide all the way to the tree. Once behind it, I whip my phone out and stare.

Song selection: "Truly Madly Deeply"

What kind of song is that?

I might have heard that song before, but I hardly re-member it.

Stupid, stupid nineties music.

Every second counts. This app thinks it's going to pull one over on me because I don't know nineties music, but it has another thing coming.

The timer is counting down from thirty seconds. This is serious business here, and I don't take winning lightly. I'm either first or last, and I won't be last. I open Google and type in the song title to get a peek at the lyrics.

"El," Stallone's husky voice calls from the other side of the trees. "Are you okay?"

My heart slams against a brick wall, and my eyes pop out of my skull. "Uh, why'd you follow me?"

"We're in the middle of the forest at night. I can't let you go wandering off. You don't have to be embarrassed that you're sick. I can take you home."

Thunk.

Thunk.

My heart slams against my rib cage at the same beat the timer counts down to my match.

I'm busted.

There's no way out of this, and I still don't know this stupid song. I will not lose.

"Look." I sidestep, coming around the tree and flipping my phone so he can see my app. "I'm not sick," I rush out as fast as I've ever spoken in my life. Hot shame floods my cheeks. "I didn't know what to say, because I spent all day singing karaoke into this app, and I'm in the championship round. It sounds stupid but I'm really competitive, and there is five hundred dollars of prize money on the line. I know it's not much, but I haven't been working all week, except for the coffee shop, but it's dead, and I've made no tips. I could really use the money, but I also didn't want to cancel our date, but I got thirty seconds until my round starts and I have to sing "Truly Madly Deeply," and I don't even know the lyrics—" I cut myself off, and a nervous giggle leaks out of my lips, as this really is the stupidest thing I've ever done. I ruined this date because of this stupid karaoke app.

His eyes glue to my phone. I'm waiting for a look of horror to flash over his face, but instead his lips bend into a smirk. "That's what this is about? Karaoke. Why didn't you say something earlier?" His giant hand flattens in front of me. "Give me the phone."

My brows furrow together for a moment before it sinks in that he's not mad at all. He has a full smile on his face, and he's ready to *help* me. "I don't think it works if you sing it. It must be my voice."

He swipes his hand through his hair. "I thought you were upset at me being so old." A giant sigh drops from his mouth, and he chuckles out loud. "If anyone can win at karaoke, it's going to be me. You hold the phone up to your mouth, but I'll sing in the background to help you find the rhythm. It's not a hard song—"

My app flashes, changing screens and I panic and cut him off, "It's starting!"

The lyrics scroll across my screen. Since I don't know them, I read them and try to find my pitch, but Stallone is right behind me, whispering the words to the melody and it helps so much. I feel dumb singing into my phone in the middle of the forest at night in front of him. Even if we make it past a first date—which I highly doubt after the way I've treated him—he'll probably never let me live this down.

My gauge quickly fills with green to indicate I'm winning. Then I no longer care how dumb I look.

I'm winning.

My confidence soars.

The headlights from the truck are the only real light, and it's enough for me to see his dark eyes staring deeply into mine. Our voices blend well together. Me, a solid soprano, and him a bass. The song ends with a long pause on the screen. I hold my breath, my gaze bouncing from Stallone to the screen. He's still here, which is mind-blowing to me, and he seems to be holding his breath, as excited as I am.

Confetti pops, and I squeal and pump my fist in the air. "We won!"

He throws his head back, letting laughter roll out, at the same time he scoops me up into a giant bear hug. It sends a whoosh right through me as our bodies are pressed together. All the air is wrung out of my lungs, and I can't help but freeze. After a complete twirl, he sets me down, and that's when I notice his nice pants are muddy. I motion to his pant legs. "How come you're all muddy?"

His smile never leaves his face. "I slipped when I was running after you." A slow chuckle starts from his lips. "I ran as fast as I could, because I thought you were dying."

My gaze slopes until I meet his, and a swelling starts in my heart. I put my hand on his forearm and stare into his eyes. Here's a man who ran through the mud to save me. When he finds out I'd been hiding this app from him, he sings Savage Garden to me.

It's all green flags for me.

"Stallone," I whisper his name. "Thank you for helping and for not being upset."

"You're welcome." His gaze softens, bright copper flecks dancing in his eyes. "I'm relieved everything is fine. I couldn't decide if you were upset that I was old or if you were sick."

"Neither of those." I let out a mischievous laugh. "I'm just broke right now and saw a way to make some cash. Now you know my secret. Plus, I'm the ultimate Karaoke Cash-oke champion."

"That's a good title to have." He holds his hand out to me, and I take it. Hand in hand, we both head toward the truck. "How about next time you want to sing karaoke though, you just tell me, and I'll take you out to a real show?"

"That sounds fun." My bottom lip rolls under my top teeth in disbelief. I got lucky with this guy. He's so fun and easygoing, yet he really was concerned when he thought I was sick. "Just know . . ." I pause and give him a challenging side eye. "You are not going to take my title from me."

"Just you wait." He throws his head back and laughs before giving me a stern look. "You think you're competitive? You haven't seen anything yet."

"I think I hear a challenge," I joke. "Care to make a bet?"

"Absolutely." We've reached the truck, and he opens my door for me, standing back while I hop in. "Not karaoke though. I get to pick the challenge, and it starts tomorrow."

My lips slide into a grin that fills my entire face. "Deal."

He shuts my door, and while I wait for him to return to the truck, my gaze drops to the ground. It's all fun to joke about, but I don't live here. It stinks to find someone I connect with so well, and I'm just going to leave.

He's quiet when he climbs in his seat and shifts the truck back into gear, steering back to town. Part of me wants to invite him back to the coffee shop for a drink and more conversation, but even though I have a key, it's not my store. I don't really know Graham or how he'd take it to have guests so late. I don't have any other ideas, and he doesn't offer anywhere else to go, driving me back to the lodge. He's quiet when he pulls into the parking lot. "Thank you for taking me out," I say as I turn to him to say goodnight. "I had a nice time, and I'm sorry for worrying you."

He slides his arm on the back of the seat, and it feels like a subtle invitation to move closer, but I'm not sure. "I had a great time too," he says as his eyes lock with mine. "If it's still okay, I'm going to text you tomorrow."

"I'd like that." I trap my bottom lip in my teeth and wait for him to say or do anything to indicate he wants me to stay, but he's still. After a quiet beat, I put my hand on the door handle, and push the door open, calling back, "Night."

"Night," he says as I shut the door, and I turn to go back into the lodge. I'm feeling a little down that the date is over. It's still fairly early, and I hope it wasn't me who made it end so soon. A tightness creeps into my chest, creating a pain in my heart different than anything I've experienced. It's like I miss him already.

THIRTEEN

Stallone

The next morning, my mind is quiet when I wake. Peaceful, and with only one thing on my mind. I can't wait to see Arielle. As soon as I'm back from walking Lucky, I turn on one stove burner. While I wait for my pan to preheat, I text her.

Me: Are you ready for a little friendly competition?

Little dots pop up on my phone screen, indicating she's typing back, and butterflies dance in my stomach in anticipation. I shuffle to the fridge for the egg carton and have enough time to crack two eggs into the pan before her reply flashes on my screen.

El: You're not going to win at karaoke.

Chuckling, I type my response.

Me: Remember, I said no karaoke. I had something more adventurous but equally competitive in mind.

Her reply is lightning fast.

El: Like what?

Me: It's a surprise. Can I pick you up after work?

El: Yes, I close at 6 again.

Me: I'll be there.

El: Should I do anything to prepare?

Me: Maybe bring some tissues for when you lose.

El: Ha! Funny. I never lose.

Me: See you in a few hours.

El: Can't wait.

I drop my phone to the counter and turn back to flip my eggs, chuckling to myself. She is just so much fun to be around. Now that we have the whole karaoke thing out in the open, I hope we can spend some real time together without so many interruptions.

I pull up to the Coffee Loft curb, and she promptly emerges, strutting over to the truck with her shoulders pulled back. When she opens the passenger door and peeps her head in, her huge messy blond bun drawing my attention, for just a moment before I level my gaze with hers. "I have no idea what you're up to." There's a chuckle braided into her words. "But I'm prepared to win." She slides into her seat and gives me a playfully haughty grin. "So you better be ready to lose."

"You think so, gorgeous? Remember, I'm the reason you won karaoke." I give her a solid thirty seconds to explain exactly how she thinks she can beat me at anything. She slowly straps the seat belt over her lap, not saying a thing, but her top lip is trapped between her teeth when she smiles. I struggle not to stare at her because she's so stunning. My pulse rockets through my veins, and I do my best to shift the truck back into drive and steer toward the mountains.

"I do think so," she finally replies, her eyes reflecting the last of the sunlight streaming in through the windshield. "I did my vocal warm-ups, my leg stretches, and I even skipped lunch in case this is an eating competition."

She could continue her smack talk, but my lips bend down from the guilt of not giving her at least a little hint. I sure didn't want her to walk around all hangry. "Not an eating competition. If you're hungry, we can grab an early dinner?"

"I'm good," she affirms, her eyes laser focused on where I'm driving to. "Depending on what the competition is, I may not want a full stomach."

I take a sharp left and steer up the narrow gravel road that leads back to my place. "I thought it would be fun to show you a little game I like to play when I'm bored at work."

"Game at work?" One of her feathered brows rises above the other until her face is a state of frozen confusion. "Aren't you a lumberjack?" The other eyebrow shoots up to match the height of the first, and she exclaims, "Tell me we are throwing axes! I've always wanted to do that."

"Oh, I don't know if I could trust you with an ax." I release one of my hands from the steering wheel and run it over my whiskers, and I teasingly give her a side-eye. Here's the thing, I've been throwing axes since I was the same height they were. There's no way she could win, but that's part of my plan. I'm going to set her up to lose, so I can win what I want.

"It's my surprise, isn't it?" She leans toward me, her eyes pleading.

"I thought it would be fun." I shrug, downplaying how excited I am to do this. "If you think you'd want to try it, I'm game to teach you."

"Oh, I'm game, but you don't have to teach me. I'm a natural at winning everything."

"We'll see about that." Pushing my tongue to the roof of my mouth, I raise my chin and take a sharp left onto the steep dirt road. The tires rattle in the worn ruts. Out of my peripheral vision, I see El casually grabbing the door handle.

"You really live out in the middle of nowhere." Her head moves in all directions as she scans the thick evergreens and steep sloped mountain banks.

"It may seem like that but it's not too far from my parents' house and my brother's. We all live on the same acreage, and it's honestly all I know. It's not that far from town, but out here in the mountains, it feels like I'm in my own world."

"It's so different from what I'm used to in Boston." Her gaze never leaves her window, and we round the last bend in the road, taking the turn to a clearing in the trees, which opens into my place. "This is not your house." Her gaze darts to me.

I press the brake to roll to a stop and shift into park in front of my garage. "I built it so I think that makes it mine."

"I thought you said you had a mountain cabin." Her gaze shifts from me to the house. "This is a mansion."

"It's bigger than I need, but I figured I was only going to build once and might as well have some room to grow." I grab my door handle and push open the door, calling back, "I can give you a tour if you want, but I'll admit about ninety percent of the house isn't even furnished yet."

She quickly hops out of the truck, and I wait for her to meet me by the walkway. We stroll up the pebbled path together. When I look over at her, walking by my side, my heart skips a beat. Usually, it's windier here than it is in town, but it's a rare moment where everything in nature is still, and to me it feels like a collective pause, as even the usually noisy birds are watching El—more than likely they are as mesmerized by her as I am. It feels awfully natural to have her next to me. Even if I am a little nervous to welcome her into my home. I never have guests, and I certainly don't entertain, but a niggling in the back of my head tells me this girl is different.

"Here's the plan." I motion to the back of the house, the side with the perfect view over the valley, where I have my practice target set up. "You can have as many practice shots as you want, but once we start the round, there's no starting over." My boots plod over the worn path. "It's not a competition unless we have a wager. What do you think we could bet?" I give her my mischievous smile, because I already know what I'm betting.

When she looks at me, it's pure magnetism, and I would probably agree to anything she'd say. My heart pounds against my rib cage, strong and steady. She hovers close by, bouncing her gaze to the target and then to me. "I don't need a practice shot." She raises her chin, appearing to analyze the target, but I suspect it's an act.

"Okay." I stare down into her eyes, and my heart flutters as I hold my breath. God made me a sizable man. It's not something I usually think about, but when I'm standing next to her, my body dwarfs hers. She's so stunning, I can't resist putting my hand on her lower back. When I'm this close to her, I just need to touch her. "And what should we bet?"

"If I win, you have to make me dinner." Her nose crinkles into the cutest pattern as she passes a sassy smile in my direction.

"I'll make you dinner if I lose." I nudge her shoulder, and I am instantly stilled by the spark that ignites in me.

"I won't complain about that." She gives me a gentle nudge back. "What happens if you win?"

So, I know what I want. I've never been so sure of something before that it's bizarre.

Standing outside my house with this woman I only recently met; a week ago, I'd have sworn I'd die a reclusive bachelor. As I stand here locked in an unwavering gaze with her, there's only one thing I want to do. It's something she put in my head days ago when she served me those sweet kiss coffees. With one brow cocked, I rub my hands together, drumming up the anticipation. "If I win," I lower my voice into a low rasp, "I get to kiss you like you're my girlfriend."

One of her hands smooths over her cheek, and she tucks her hand into her wild heap of hair, all the while her cheeks fire a bright pink wave. "El," I say softly, my tongue heavy, and her lack of reply causes my stomach to knot. "If you don't want—"

"Bet." She extends her hand like this is a boardroom negotiation. I take her hand in mine, knowing I'm going to win. This is clearly a setup. As I search her face for clues of unease, there are none. If anything, her gaze heats, and I'd say she's having as much fun as I am.

"Ladies first," I say through playfully gritted teeth.

She drops my hand, planting both of her palms on her hips with a take-charge expression on her face and impatiently looks at me. "Where's my ax?"

Whoa, now that's not an expression you want to hear from a woman every day.

It's wild but yet hot.

I walk to the porch where I keep several of my best throwing axes on a stand and run my hand along the row until I get to the lightest one. Her cyan-blue eyes track me as I walk the ax down to her and hand it over. "Can I walk you through a toss?"

She grabs the ax with both hands, her lips curling as she scrutinizes the ax. "This will do."

There's just enough of the sunset left to give us the light we need, and I stand back a few feet and hold my hands up to walk her through the motion. "First, you want to look at your target and never take your eyes off it. Then you raise your arms up slowly, keep your ax steady, and be careful not to drop it behind you."

She mimics my actions and then sets her gaze back on the target. My heart is ramming against my chest, and everything rolls out in slow motion. Her form is decent, but I still flinch when she releases the ax. It sails across the yard, snagging the target on the bottom right. "Not bad." I push my bottom lip out, pretending to be impressed.

Her face is a blend of doubt and triumph, and she steps to the side. "Your turn."

I rub my hands together again, teasing her. "Time to watch and learn." To make it fair, I walk up to the target, take her ax out and return it to the porch. I retrieve the heaviest one for myself and turn back to the target. "I'll stand way back here to give you the advantage." This is like taking candy from a baby. She must know this is a setup. I stand back, stretching both ways at the waist, building up the anticipation for her.

One firm toss across the yard, and I'll finally know what it feels like to have those sweet lips on mine.

My gaze wafts to her, and a beaming smile is spread across her gorgeous face. Shoot. Her button dimple on her cheek is even creased. My stomach wooshes. I'm such a sucker for dimples.

"What are you waiting for?" She bats her lashes at me, and I swear her dimple winks.

"Ah, nothing." I square my feet to the target and raise my ax, but a wave of guilt washes over me. I instantly lower the ax and turn toward her. I was only trying to impress her, but this isn't right. "Look, this clearly isn't a fair bet. I'm going to win."

Her bright eyes shine up at me, and the smile on her perfect-kissable lips doesn't deflate. If anything, they appear to plump up more, enticing me in. I can almost feel her sweet pink flesh when she lowers her voice, "That was always the point." She gives me a nonchalant side-eye, and the twinkle that sparks out of the corners of her eyes tells me she was here for the kiss too.

A shot of electricity shoots straight through my chest and doesn't stop until it zaps my heart, firing all my insides. My brain shuts off, and a pull of gravity draws my gaze back to her mouth. Her eyes widen, and I can't help act but out of pure instinct when she bats her lashes. She strides over to me. Even with her shoulders back, she's still at least a foot shorter than me. She doesn't stop until she's fully in my wide space bubble, close enough to nudge my elbow. "You know if you quit, not only am I going to think you suck, but I'm going to tell everyone you lost."

"Everyone? You don't know anyone here," I puff out, enjoying her sass. She's standing so near me, the heat of her body wafts off her, engulfing me, and makes it impossible to think about anything else than how perfectly kissable those lips are.

She's so close, I could lower my head straight down and land perfectly on her lips. She's unwavering, not backing up even a toe. She's practically begging for this kiss. I twist my lips into a line of flirtation and lower my head, speaking low, "I just need to make sure you aren't going to hold a grudge when I win, because I always hit my target."

A visible swallow rises and lowers in her throat, and she holds my gaze level with so much potency, adrenaline flits through my veins. I love the feel of her gaze on me, and coupled with the heat permeating off her body, there's so much magnetism drawing me closer. "No grudges." Her words release me from our hold, and I remember I'm holding an ax.

The way she smiles has my heart slamming against my rib cage. She has to know what's coming, and she clearly wants this as much as I do. I take a safety step to the side to clear space between us, and raise my ax. My hands warm as a blush flutters through my whole body in anticipation. I don't even need to watch, the ax lands in the perfect middle of the target.

I turn toward her, ready to feast my eyes on her beautiful smile. I shake my head, backing out of the competition. "It really wasn't fair," I say, but before I can continue, she closes the space between us. A hand snakes around my neck, and she pulls me down to her while she rises to the tips of her toes.

It's fast.

It's a little bit feral.

My heart expands, drinking her in as her body comes even closer.

Her lips capture mine, and she takes all the breath I have, erasing every ounce of insecurity I had over this bet. I wasn't taking advantage of her any more than she was of me. It's confirmed even more when I feel her smile into our kiss. Whatever this is, it's mutual. When she pulls away, she leaves me standing with my mouth dropped open.

"So much for being just friends." I reach up and physically close my mouth with my hand. "At least we got the hard part out of the way."

A serious line pins between her brows as she gazes back at me. I hold my breath as I wait impatiently to hear what she has to say.

She can't be mad.

She kissed me.

Her lips purse out, and I bite my cheek, waiting.

"Maybe it was meant to happen." A simple gesture follows, where she grabs my hand, pushing her fingers between mine, and smiles sweetly at me. My heart swells, feeling her hand in mine, and her gaze so steady on me it's as if she has nowhere else to go. "Now, let's see about that dinner you promised me."

FOURTEEN

Arielle

Stallone leads the way inside his house, and I struggle to keep my face neutral. This entire mountain is steeped so strongly in evergreen scent, and it doesn't dissipate when I pass through the threshold. More forest fumes waft around me as I take in his home. The exterior design resembles something similar to a log cabin, only so huge it could pass as a small lodge. Now, I see there is nothing rustic about the interior. It has dark wood floors and an open floor plan that leads to a modern kitchen, complete with stainless steel appliances and granite countertops. The wall across from the kitchen is replaced by floor-to-ceiling windows, opening to a view of the valley below. The window's so large, when I stand next to it, I feel like I'm standing outside. I step right up to the window and look down, scanning all along the valley. "This is a stunning view."

"It's my favorite thing about this place." He comes up beside me, his frame so huge I have to tip my head all the way to look up at him. His shoulders span wide and appear even broader, as his arms are so large he can't lower them to his body. Yet, I don't feel small standing next to him. If anything, it feels safe and shielded. Protected. He holds a lingering gaze on me that melts me to the floor. Ever since he brought up kissing me like his girlfriend, I find myself imagining what it would be like to be his girlfriend.

I can't imagine feeling any other emotions but loved and protected.

"What would you like for dinner?" He hikes a thumb over his shoulder, back toward the kitchen. "I have steak and beef thawed out."

"Oh." I pinch my lips together, as I love teasing him. "I only eat fish and chicken."

His eyes spring wide, and he starts a rebuttal, "I can make a vegetable stew—"

"I was kidding." I chuckle and clench his forearm, drawing myself a little closer to him. Man, it's strong and sinewy. I could certainly get used to these. "If you have beef, burgers are great."

"That's my specialty." He gives me a playful wink and crosses the room.

I back away from the window as well, following him to the kitchen. "What can I help with?"

"How about a salad?"

"I can do that." I gesture to the oversized fridge. "Can I take a peek?"

"Go right ahead." He opens the fridge, grabs a package of beef and holds on to the door until I come forward. I find the lettuce and cucumbers in the crisper and set them on the counter. A knife block sets next to me, so I pull out a smaller knife and locate the cutting board that pulls out from the counter. I pivot and set about washing the produce when Stallone fills in the silence, "So, we suck at being just friends, huh?"

I sputter out a laugh, but my heart doesn't think it's funny. It's the kind of laugh you have when you aren't sure what to say or think. "You started it with that bet."

"Not me." He shakes his head back and forth while he unwraps the beef. "You started it days ago with your sweet kiss coffee."

"What?" I pretend to be offended by lowering my brow and tilting my head away. "That was just coffee."

"Coffee with all the innuendo?" His gaze traps mine, and I don't turn away.

"Maybe." I shrug and raise my head to the cupboards above me.

As if reading my mind, he opens one, pulls out a bowl, and sets it in front of me. "Maybe?" His raised eyebrow challenges me. "Then you asked me to stay late first."

"I did." I nod and move the veggies to the bowl with my hands. "And I'm not the least bit sorry I did that."

He straightens his smile, boring a gaze into mine that seems to go right through me. "Tell me about your life back home."

"That's a weird thing to change the subject to."

"Not really." His tone is curt. "You're going back there tomorrow. Aren't you?"

"I-I am supposed to." All my replies fire out rapidly as a defensiveness rises in my chest.

"Answer my question. Are you going back tomorrow?" His voice is firm and insistent.

"Ah." A vision forms in my brain, bringing forth all the things that are in my life in Boston.

Tom. Definitely don't care to see him anymore.

My dad. He wouldn't be happy if I left Boston, but he couldn't stop me.

My job. I'm not even sure I have it anymore because I haven't showed up for days.

None of those things are enough to take me from the gaze that Stallone has on me now. When he looks at me, I feel like the most beautiful woman on the planet, and all I want to do is melt into his arms. It's more than just feeling beautiful though. I feel seen and respected, so much more than I have ever. My thoughts are muted but insistent with the biggest thing being that we both agreed from the start we weren't looking for anything long term.

"Would it matter if I didn't?" I level my gaze with his, and he wraps his arm around my waist, pulling me toward him with so much insistence I must place my palms on his chest to keep my balance. His hand finds my chin, tipping my face up with the same urgency, and his lips crash down on mine, leaving no room in my heart for doubts. When he pulls away, my fingertips rise to brush over my bottom lip that's still tingling. I wait for him to say anything to hint of how he's feeling.

When he speaks it doesn't disappoint. "It could matter."

I swallow, feeling my upcoming decision deep in my gut. I know what I want to do. I stare off past him, trying to think of what I'm going to tell my family. It's not even so much my dad, but Christian. He's so insanely protective of me, and when he finds out the reason I want to stay, he's going to chew fire.

Fifteen

Stallone

"I know you love coffee." I bring her a mug of the piping hot coffee I had made as we move to the couch for after-dinner conversations. She takes her mug, and I plop down beside her, taking up so much room, it feels like a love seat.

I'm not complaining.

We ate our burgers side by side, bellied up on my kitchen island. She didn't miss a chance to brush my shoulder or reach out to give me a soft touch. It's more than the flirtation we've shared before. Those little touches do everything to ignite a fire in my heart and bond me to her.

"You make great coffee." She hums between several slow swallows and focuses on the after the nightly news talk show that's on TV.

"It's the Keurig," I reply, but then our conversation wanes. The longer our date goes on, the more comfortable we are sitting in silence. It doesn't surprise me one bit when she slouches her body against mine, pulling her feet up under her until we are fully snuggling. I wrap my arms around her and it's a relief to feel her this close. She's relaxed, not the hyper- competitive woman she was on our first date. I take the moment to lean over and drop a kiss on top of her head. Her sweet honey scent consumes me, and I marvel at how I'm one lucky guy.

Speaking of Lucky, I let him in the house after dinner, and he took right to El, curling up on the floor by our feet. The three of us are the picture of happiness I always had in my head. Only now I finally see El's face in that picture, and it makes my heart pound so hard that if I didn't know it was happiness, I would think I was having a medical emergency.

I grab her free hand and playfully rub my thumb over hers. "So, what's your family going to say when they find out you met an old man?"

She tips her face up to mine. "You're not an old man, and it doesn't matter what they think. It only matters what I think."

The thing is, I want to believe her.

But she's so young.

Some would say too young, with wild oats left to sow.

But I believe her when she says she doesn't care, because she doesn't seem the type to care about sowing wild oats.

I'm in that place in life where I'm ready to make adjustments for someone special. I'm not so stubborn to think life must only be my way. If she wants to go slow, we will tiptoe together, relishing all the milestones we make. If she wants to move things along faster, and wants a family with me . . .

Then I'm an even luckier man.

I've never felt so still inside while knowing it's all going to work out.

I roll my bottom lip, trapping it in my teeth. It's crazy to feel this way so soon after just meeting someone, but I've never felt this kind of connection with anyone.

I'd say I'm falling for her.

It's clearly too soon to tell her that, but I have something else in mind. Something to show her.

"Hey." I drop my hand down to her hip and lean forward at the same time. "Come with me."

Her perfect brow furrows together into a quizzical look, but she doesn't hesitate to follow my lead. We rise off the couch together, and I take her hand and lead her to the French doors off the kitchen and onto the wraparound deck. I don't need to tell her why I brought her out here. The ladylike gasp that slips from her lips the second she sees the sky tells me she gets it.

"I've never seen stars like this before." Her tone is drenched in awe as her gaze glues upward, while she meanders all the way over to the end of the deck that overlooks the valley. Nothing blocks her view, and her expression morphs into one of childlike wonder.

I knew the stars wouldn't disappoint as the sky was cloudless all day. Normally, when I'm out at night, I enter a haze where I can't help but think this must be the most beautiful place on earth. Tonight, I just look at her. I walk up behind her and wrap both arms around her body. She doesn't flinch, but covers her hands with mine, and we freeze together looking up. She fits so perfectly into my arms that my heart skips an actual beat, making my chest ache, and I suck back a deep breath.

I never planned on Arielle.

I certainly wasn't out looking for something to consume my thoughts so much that it makes it impossible for me to concentrate on anything for longer than a few minutes, but I'm not going to run from this either. I dip my head down to rest it on top of hers.

"This is absolutely breathtaking," she coos after many long moments of silence. "I can tell why you love it here so much."

"One of the many reasons." The view from here never gets old, but a tinge of jealousy buds in my chest, as I can't help but wish I could see it for the first time again. Yet, I'm so grateful I can share it with her. "I grew up on the top of this same mountain. When I was a kid, I used to imagine that the stars would start to fall, and since I was so close, I'd be able to just reach up and catch one."

"I can see why. It does feel like we're right there with them. You're really lucky to live here." She turns her head, scanning in all directions, while pulling in a deep inhalation. "The air out here is so clean and crisp. I'm going to miss that too."

"I'm assuming it's completely different than what you have in Boston."

She answers me by squeezing my hands tighter, and I can feel her body slouch even more onto mine, creating a oneness that feels flawless. I would call this perfection. If there is anything I can do to get her to stay, even just a little while longer, I'm going to do it. I'm not the smartest guy on the planet, but I know a woman like Arielle is rare. Chemistry like ours is even rarer. "El," I rasp over the top of her head when my emotions bubble up so much, I can no longer contain them.

"Yeah." Her voice is soft and dreamy, like she's dreaming the things I refuse to let myself dream about. Like how I don't want her to leave, ever. In my head I see this play out like a movie. She leaves her place in Boston to stay here with me. It doesn't take me more than a second to make her my entire world, and it's not more than a month or two before we get married. I wouldn't be surprised if we had a little one on the way this time next year. That's the life I want so badly, but I don't dare to tell her that much.

"One thing I've learned in life is sometimes you have to take chances." I stall, take a deep breath, but that inhalation only pulls her sweet scent into my lungs, and it makes my knees shake. I risk another kiss, just ghosting my lips over the crown of her head, and I pray it's not the last time I get to do that. Swallowing, I say one mere sentence, but it's so powerful I feel as if I'm pouring my whole heart out to her, and my heart slams against my chest. "I hope this doesn't scare you, because we haven't known each other very long, but I'm falling for you."

I hold my breath, expecting a long pause and maybe even a little squirming, because I know I can come on strong, but I won't dance around for what I want. She does nothing of the sort. Instead, she turns around, her head tipped back so she can look all the way up at me, and she says with bold confidence, "I'm falling for you too."

I wouldn't believe something like this could happen so fast, but at that moment a seal is created in my heart, locking it off from anyone else but her.

Sixteen

Arielle

The next morning, I'm still in a haze of overflowing emotions from my date with Stallone, but I make it to the coffee shop right on time. While flipping the closed sign to open, a royal-blue streak running down the sidewalk catches my attention.

Christian.

In a blue warm-up suit, like the kind that was popular in the eighties.

Not his best look.

Pushing the door open a crack, I call out, "Hey, the eighties called. They want their clothes back."

"Funny." He gives me a pointed look and continues to stride forward.

"I told you I don't need a babysitter." My lips curl against my will, because even though he's here to take me home, it's still good to see him.

His knees rise to a ridiculously high angle as he marches forward until he grabs the door from my hand, pushing his way inside. "I'm not here to babysit you. I did a bunch of phone interviews for the manager's job. One of them is coming in for a second interview in person today. I think he's going to work out perfectly."

Christian's gangly legs cross over the threshold before I do, and he scans the place. "Graham never came back to work?"

"He's been coming in for an hour or two in the late mornings to check on things. He says he won't be returning full time until next week."

Continuing to make his way back to the coffee bar, Christian's gaze freezes on my roses, still soaking in the coffeepot. "What's going on with this decorating monstrosity?"

I quicken my steps and slide in front of the vase, hiding them from his view. "It's not decorating. They were a gift, and I didn't have a vase."

"Oh, no!" He sidesteps, reaching his hand around me, trying to get to the vase, but I push him back with my palm while he rants, "That dirty rotten Tom is not going to have his cursed flowers in my shop—"

"They are not from Tom!" I use both hands to hold him back. "I met someone."

His body goes stiff, no longer pushing forward while his gaze slides to me, a suspicious gleam sparkling out of the corner of his eye. "Tell me he's not a giant loser."

"He's not a loser at all." My brows furrow together, and anger bubbles in my gut. I hate that Christian treats me like I don't know how to make my own decisions. "He's a perfect gentleman, and you met him already."

"I met him?" he echoes, his hands planting on his hips. "Who are you even talking about?"

"You saw him here. That man who came in with the flannel shirt and beard."

Christian's jaw dramatically flops down. "Tell me you're kidding."

My cheeks are hot, but I don't back down. "We got to talking, and he asked me out on a date, and we really enjoy being around each other."

"El! How can I ever trust you?" His eyes roll to the ceiling before they slam back at me. "I leave you alone for a few days, thinking nothing could possibly go wrong, but you somehow manage to start dating an ogre."

"An ogre?" My head jolts back as I'm offended for Stallone. "That's awfully mean and shallow of you."

"Why?" Christian's eyes bug out of his head. "You just got out of a horrendous relationship. Why would you do this?" He gestures forward, demanding I speak, but then adds, "Oh, wait, is that what this is? A rebound thing? Something to even the score with Tom?"

"No." I struggle to put into words what happened these last few days. "This has nothing to do with Tom. I know it sounds weird, but Stallone and I have made a connection, and it feels like I've known him my whole life."

"Stallone?" Christian snarls his lip and acts like he's going to vomit by dropping his jaw. "Is that even his real name?"

"Stop." My voice is quieter than usual, as I don't have it in me to argue with Christian over a guy he's never even spoken to. The front door swings open, and Graham shuffles through with two sacks in front of him. I'm grateful for the interruption, planting my attention on him. "Did you find a good sale?"

"Diapers," he huffs and heaves the sacks onto the bookstore checkout counter. "And a bag of cabbage. Apparently, that helps with nursing 'issues.'" He makes finger quotes while shaking his head, and then drops his hands to rifle through some papers on his desk, pulling out an invoice on the bottom. He advances toward his computer and clicks the mouse to turn it on, while adding, "I need to double-check something that was bothering me."

"How's the baby?" I ask, already feeling the stress wafting off him.

"He's really great." Graham's gaze stays fixed on his computer; a smile never leaves his face. "He's healthy, and

I feel blessed everything has gone well. How are things here?"

"Great." I nod, even though he's not looking at me. Christian cuts me off before I can expound.

"Interesting." He parks his hand on his hip again as that seems to be his new favorite place to rest it. "It's been really interesting. I was back in New York for a few days, and El here has started dating someone. Do you know anything about some stupidly named Stallone guy?"

"Christian," I scold, but they both ignore me, as Graham is also happy to gossip in front of me.

"Stallone Hart from Hart Logging?" Graham's gaze cuts to meet mine.

"Sure." Christian locks on Graham with his impatient glare. "We will go with that. Who is he?"

My face burns, and I feel like a small child whose parents need to discuss my inappropriate behavior in front of them.

Only I did nothing wrong.

Graham's slow shrug draws out the suspense, while Christian and I both stare at him, waiting. "Stallone's been a regular here for as long as I've been here. Not much of a talker. I've always seen him as a loner. I'm surprised he went out with you. How'd you get him to do that?"

"He asked me." I stare forward, feeling like that should be obvious.

"Interesting." Graham stuffs his invoice back into a file drawer and returns his gaze with a thoughtful expression. "You do know he's super rich, right?"

"Not really." I'm definitely not going to admit to Christian right now that I've been to his mansion. He'd come unglued.

"Yeah, he's made a fortune with his wood business. Course, it was his dad's before his, and if I remember the rumors I've heard correctly, it might have actually even been his granddad's company first. He seems like a good guy," Graham says with thoughtful inflections. "I'm just surprised he asked you out, because he seemed to be over dating after his last breakup . . ." Graham's voice trails off while he opens another file drawer and runs his hands over the top of it looking for something. When he finds what he wants, he grabs it and closes the drawer.

Christian doesn't wait for us to have privacy. His gaze slams back to me and he lets out a noisy huff. "Seriously, El, please tell me this is all a joke about this guy."

"You don't want me to be happy?" I'm not even trying to argue. It's absurd he thinks he gets an opinion about this. I went on two dates with the guy. That's it. It's not a big deal. It's not like we eloped. A naughty chuckle bubbles in my gut as I visualize how fun it would be to tease Christian that Stallone and I eloped.

"Of course you're not happy." He gestures forward wildly. "You just went through a horrific breakup. This is just a distraction." He squares his stance, his face transforms into a stoic expression. "Trust me, El. What you need is to come back with me and spend some time healing and don't go on any dates for at least a month, or two."

I try to set my mind on Tom, but it won't stay there. I can't even think about him if I want to. This has nothing to do with Tom or what I recently went through. I don't know how to convince Christian of that.

My nervous gaze pulls to Graham. He's more thoughtful as he overhears our conversation, but he doesn't back away when he catches me looking at him. "What do you think?" The question is out of my mouth before I can second-guess allowing an almost-stranger into my personal life.

His brows raise as he hangs onto my gaze, and he asks, "About Stallone?"

"Maybe it's about him," I bumble around for words, "but it's also about me and what I want. I don't want to go back to Boston. I like it here, and yes, okay..." My voice rises as I circle back to my earlier thought. It appears my thoughts are growing less cloudy by the second. "Maybe, by doing what I want, I can say it's about Stallone. So, what if I want to get to know him more? That doesn't make me a bad person."

"Whoa, I never said it did." His kind chuckle erases some of the tension. "I just wanted to make sure I knew what we were talking about." He lowers his gaze to his papers, moving them into a straight pile. His voice is firm when he asks, "Do you think you could love him?"

"Whoa, whoa, whoa. Don't say that!" Christian butts in, physically inserting himself between us with his eyes glued to me. "You don't have to answer that. That's a dumb question." He flashes a look of annoyance at Graham. "Of course she doesn't love him. They just met."

"I didn't ask if she loved him. I asked if she *could*. There's a clear difference." Graham crosses his arms against his chest, seeming to stand even taller. "I met my wife when I was in high school. We didn't find a way to be together for many years, but in our years apart, I always knew I *could* love her if I was given the chance. I knew it from the first time I saw her."

"You're not helping," Christian mumbles, turning his back to Graham. When he looks at me, my chin quivers. I know exactly what Graham is saying. I'm not that inexperienced to say it's love, but every part of my heart twists when I think of him. I am certain if I gave it a chance, I could love him. "El," Christian's coax is softer this time, as his gaze paces my face which I know is not hiding my emotions. When I say nothing, he repeats softer, "El."

I step forward, sharing all my vulnerabilities with him and whisper, "I think I can."

His eyes take an arc roll before he grunts, "So, what are you telling me? You want me to leave you here?"

I shrug, completely unsure what the days before me will offer, but I know I must try. "I'm saying I want to stay for a while. I actually think I'd enjoy being a barista. It has to be better than working for dad. You don't have to hire anyone. At least not now. It works out that I can stay here and see what this thing is."

"You're for real about this?" he says, voice oddly quieter, and it's evident this is finally sinking in for him.

"I am."

"Okay, then." He shakes his head, backing away. "I'll finish this week's order, but then I'll leave the rest up to you." The thing with Christian is, he's always been dramatic, but something happened when he met Portia. He gained a sense of urgency where when they are not together, he just seems edgy. I know the impatience he shows me is because he really is in a hurry to tie up his ends here to get home to her. It was never his plan to leave me here, and it is unsettling to him.

What he doesn't know is, the same urgency he always has to return to Portia is one that now pounds in my chest. As I sit here at the coffee shop with a full day before me, all I can think about is getting off work so I can see Stallone.

That's not love.

But it's something.

And I can't wait to see what it turns out to be.

Seventeen

Stallone

I clear my throat for the second time as I stand outside the coffee shop. The sign has already been switched to closed for the night. Through the window, I can see El is alone again, but for the life of me I can't go inside.

With her hair up in one of the wild messy buns, that always leaves a few wispy strands to fall down to frame her face, she floats around the coffee bar, wiping off the counter. Her expression is soft, and under the muted Coffee Loft lights, her skin has a soft glow. I catch my breath in the back of my throat as I marvel at how she's absolutely ravishing.

Never in my life did I think a woman like her would have eyes for someone like me. I reach out to grab the door handle but freeze again. This is so different than the other days

I met El at work. Before it was a mere flirtation. Something changed yesterday. Now I feel like I have something to lose. It's so early in this situationship for me to ask for her to give anything up. We hardly know each other. Yet, the magnetism has only grown stronger. My palms tremble as I finally find the bravery and pull open the door. I heave a sigh of relief that she left it unlocked. She was clearly waiting for me.

At least, I hope.

Her gaze locks on mine, and if I didn't know better, I'd say it's a tad frantic. "Stallone."

Man, I love the way my name sounds when it falls from her lips. Her one-word greeting is enough to make my heart slam against my rib cage. "Hey, gorgeous."

Her palms find the coffee bar in front of her, and she playfully leans forward while batting those gorgeous dark lashes at me. "What can I get you?"

"You know what I want." I stride forward, my steps growing longer the closer I get to her. "I came for one of your sweet kisses."

She doesn't flinch or pretend to not understand. Her gaze softens even more as she steps out from behind the bar, and she rushes forward to meet me halfway. I scoop her up in one swift motion, lifting her off the ground, and her lips find mine with perfect rhythm. The coffee shop could implode into a giant fire, and I wouldn't even notice as my eyes turn into literal hearts, and the only thing I'm able to focus on is her.

When I set her down, her eyes stay locked on me. She teasingly smiles and says, "Is that what you had in mind?"

"That'll do." Pushing my lower lip out, I nod. "But I might need seconds in a little bit."

Her soft giggles cushion my heart, and she pivots on her heel back to the bar. "Did you actually want a coffee too? I'd love to spend some time together."

"If you have time." It's an uncertain reply, and my voice cracks as I feel nauseous just coming flat out and asking her if she's leaving. She has a whole life outside of this place, and she told me from the start that she wasn't looking for anything.

She turns toward me, grabs both of my hands, and stares up at me. The lighter hue of blue fires sparkles out of her eyes. "I have time. I told Christian I was staying for at least a little while. I definitely want to see where this goes." Her tone is plumb full of certainty. "Unless you're busy." Her gaze hovers over mine, and nervous reflections shine back at me.

Was she afraid I didn't want her to stay anymore?

"El," I speak as boldly as I can, "I have all the time in the world for you. There's nowhere else I'd rather be." I move in close, wrapping my arms all the way around her into a tight embrace, and slowly lower my face down to her, ready for another kiss.

Thud.

Thud.

Ugh. I moan in my head.

I don't even have to look to know who's there, but both our gazes pull to the front window. Someone is watching us—or should I say—watching El. Lucky has jumped out of my truck again, and his nose is pressed against the glass, eyes locked on El. "Not again," I whine.

I swipe my hand through my hair and look back at El. "I think someone else is happy you're staying too."

Her eyes pump so much power over me, I am frozen when she says, "So we agree? We're going to see what happens. One day at a time . . ."

So that's how this goes...slowly, but promises of heaven just by being near her.

"I'll give you any day you want, but I think we need to do it a little differently."

She swallows before she replies with a now shaky breath, "What do you mean?"

I take a grandiose step forward, leaving no space between us and no room for doubting. "I think we should take this one sweet kiss at a time."

My hand finds her hip. She rises to the tip of her toes, clenches my shirt in a way that steals my breath, and she tugs on it, pulling me down. We find each other with perfect timing, and I close my eyes, melting into her softness. There isn't any way for this situationship to get better than this. I'm going to spend each day proving to her she made the best decision to stay here by showering her with all the kisses and affection she could ever want.

My lips pull tight as they tease a smile, but I don't break our lip-lock.

Thud

Thud.

El breaks out into a giggle, and pulls back, "Let Lucky in. I'm sure I can find him a pup cup."

I give her a pointed stare, as I'm not sure she has any idea what she's started here with Lucky. This could surely turn into a habit. "Are you sure you really want to do that?"

"Yeah." She nods a slow confirmation, adding a wink. "We have something to celebrate."

"Okay, coffees for everyone, but don't you dare give him caffeine." I stride back to the door, bracing it open for Lucky. He doesn't wait for the invite as he barrels through the door and goes right to El.

Eighteen

Arielle

Just two weeks later

"Hold your oar out in front of you like this." Stallone straightens his arms, shoulder width apart, and continues calling back his instructions from his place in front of the kayak. "Turn it gently like you're pedaling a bike with your hands." I lift my oar, mimicking his moves, ungracefully smacking the side of the kayak with my oar. "Smaller movements," he coaches as his oar grazes over the smooth river water, and we glide forward.

Correcting my pattern, I try to steady my oar, but I'm all over the place. "This is a lot harder than it looks." A chuckle leaks out of my mouth right as I tap the kayak again.

"You'll get the hang of it."

I sit back on my legs, tipping my head back to see the top of the nearby mountain. Everything is still snowcapped, and I wouldn't have believed they would be even more beautiful from this view on the water. It's what my father used to call January thaw. A nice random day in the coldest month of the year, where it's actually nice enough to go outside without a coat. Stallone picked me up from work with only one thing on his mind. Well, maybe two. He didn't forget to kiss me hello.

"So, this morning on the way to work"—Stallone's voice takes an even tone, and I lean forward, hanging on to his every word— "Ryson asked me what happened to me."

"What do you mean what happened? What's wrong?"

"Nothing's wrong." He continues to propel the kayak smoothly along the water with ease and precision. "That's what he was hinting at. He said I changed, and I told him about you."

"You did . . ." And just like that my heart crawls up in my throat with all the nerves. Stallone and I have been spending all our time together—just the two of us. One thing we haven't done is complicate things by including extra people. Sure, Christian knows about us, but it's not like I tell him personal things. I could. I trust Christian more than anyone, but it's more about protecting my heart. I'm still so confused as to what we are. "What did you say?"

"I said that I met someone, and we've been spending a lot of time together. He asked me if you were my girl-friend."

"What did you say?" I struggle not to squeak because I'm actually quite curious too. It's not a term we've used yet.

"I said, 'She lets me kiss her like she's my girlfriend.'"

My lips spread wide across my face, and I shake my head. "That's really all you care about, isn't it?" Our laughter synchronizes for a beat before it falls away, and we are left with only the soft whooshing of the oars in the water. "I ah, had an interesting conversation today too."

"Oh yeah?" He tilts his head back ninety degrees trying to sneak a side-eye on me.

"Yeah, Graham asked if I wanted to rent the apartment above the bookstore."

"He did?" He hangs on to the word did, dragging it out to last at least three syllables. "What did you say?"

"Well, I asked for a tour, and he let me take a look. It's small and very outdated, but he only wants six hundred for it. He said I can go month to month." I swallow, feeling the hugeness of this announcement deep in the pit of my stomach. "I told him I'd take it."

"Are you for real?" He twists in the kayak as best he can, meeting his gaze directly with mine. "You're moving here?"

"If you want me to…" I love looking into his eyes. They don't make brown eyes like that anymore. Full and honest, bearing so many emotions in the reflections that never disappoint.

"W-well, y-yeah." He seems to stutter a bit before his words come out. "I want that more than anything. You know what that means."

I tap my finger to his chin, holding it there in pause. "Ah, it means you are invited to help me move all my stuff."

I linger on how it's crazy his smile is both serious and teasing at the same time. "Absolutely I can help you move, but if you move here, I can't continue kissing you like you're my girlfriend. That's seriously messed up."

"What?" My eyebrows bead together as I know he's setting me up for a punchline. I already know what it is, and it makes my heart beat fast.

"It means you *are* obviously my girlfriend."

"I agree." I smile sweetly and lower my lashes. I've been waiting to make this official. It's exactly what I've wanted, and I couldn't have asked for a sweeter way to be asked. I can't help but feel my life is unfolding exactly the way I dreamed it would.

Dear Reader,

Thank you for reading Truly, Madly, Steeply Brew.

I wanted to add a note to say, if you enjoyed Graham, he has his own story already. You can find it on Amazon, and it's called *Kissed by My Billionaire Boss*.

If you missed Christian and Portia's Story, that one is *Pardon My French Press*.

Introducing Mountain Brew

The Coffee Loft is back with another collection of cozy, stand-alone sweet romcoms—this time served with an extra shot of rugged charm!

Wrap yourself in flannel, breathe in the crisp mountain air, and settle in with a new brew. Mountain Brew is bold and smooth, just like the men who drink it.

These bearded mountain men may look rough around the edges, but one taste, and they're *irresistibrew!* Get ready to fall for flawed but lovable heroes, laugh-out-loud dating disasters, mixed signals, surprising twists, and heart-stopping grand gestures guaranteed to make you swoon. Grab your favorite table over in the corner and prepare to be swept off your feet by these unforgettable mountain men.

Find the series here: https://books.bookfunnel.com/t hecoffeeloftseriesmountainbrewcollection

Do you want to see what other books we have in this series? We have two more series to enjoy. Find them below:

Fall Collection: https://www.amazon.com/dp/B0CX QBFPHK

Winter Collection: https://www.ama-zon.com/dp/B0CG2MQP2J

About J.P. Sterling

J.P. Sterling grew up watching old reruns of Lucille Ball and Mary Tyler Moore and fell in love with wholesome entertainment and slapstick comedy. She loves leaning into the over-the-top humor and full circle moments, especially if it means the underdog gets to shine.

Aside from writing, she's also a wife and homeschooling mom, a holistic dietitian, a former college professor and lover of all-things dark chocolate.

*No swears. Just kisses. No Blasphemies. *

Let's get social!

Hey you amazing reader! You are invited to join my private reader group for all-things clean books and friends.

Enter the group here: https://www.facebook.com/groups/1500850764081965

Other places to follow me:

Instagram: https://www.instagram.com/stories/authorjpsterling/

Facebook: https://www.facebook.com/jpsterlingauthor/

Amazon: https://www.amazon.com/stores/author/B01N9TJXJN/about

Also by J.P. Sterling

Royally Rugged

Bosses and Billionaires Series (<u>All Standalones</u>)

Maid for my Billionaire Boss

Upcycling My Rig-Pig Boss

Kissed by My Billionaire Boss

Marooned with My Celebrity Boss

<u>A Heart that Dances Series</u>

Dancing on Broken Ankles

The Stars We See

A Heart that Dances

A Heart that Loves

<u>Water and Stone Duet</u>

Ruby in the Water

Lily in the Stone